## "WE MEET AGAIN"

Matt found no rest that night. The sounds of the horses whinnying in the corral drew his attention, and he knew without thinking that he had visitors.

Five horsemen charged through the river, howling and firing rifles. Matt opened up with both pistols. One rider was flung from his horse, and a second screamed in pain.

Then One Eye rode forward and waved the others back.

For a moment the bare-chested leader remained in the shallows, staring at Matt with cold hatred. Moonlight illuminated the scarred bronze face. The two of them gazed across the open ground, their cold, hard eyes examining each other for some sign of weakness. . . .

# MATT RAMSEY

## WILL McLENNAN

JOVE BOOKS, NEW YORK

MATT RAMSEY

A Jove Book/published by arrangement with
the author

PRINTING HISTORY
Jove edition/November 1989

ISBN: 0-515-10175-3

10  9  8  7  6  5  4  3  2  1

# CHAPTER

# ★ 1 ★

No one really set out for Buffalo Springs. The odd huddle of clapboard grog houses and gaming tents huddled around a trading post midway between the frontier town of Jacksboro and the Red River. Hunters exchanged hides for powder, shot, and such supplies as couldn't be dug from the ground or carved from bone. Cattlemen driving longhorns north to Kansas sometimes stocked larders or satisfied a thirst in the dusty town. It was a place to be passed through . . . or by. No one stayed.

Matt Ramsey knew that kind of town well. Since the war, he'd wandered across half of northern Texas, collecting maverick longhorns to goad north into Kansas or chasing down herds of range mustangs. He was an unsettled sort, and he never stuck anyplace for long. Some called him a wayward soul. Others said his feet got the itch to move on. Whatever it was, Matt wasn't a man to find himself in the same county two summers running.

That early spring of '68 he was in Buffalo Springs. Another year, another season, and it would have been somewhere else. Fate had her way of sweeping a man where and when she chose, and Matt gave little thought to his destiny anymore. The war and the hard years that had followed snatched away what pur-

1

pose had once filled him with resolve. Beneath his sour-lipped frown, the shaggy brown hair and unshaven chin, there lurked the cold soul of a man eaten up by bitterness. His ragged trousers and dirty buckskin jacket testified to hard times. The deep blue eyes half concealed by the shadow of his hat brim issued that mixture of menace and warning that might have said here was a man better left to himself.

Shabby or not, Matt stepped through the door of Walker West's trading post with the long gait of a man better than six feet tall. His shoulders remained broad, though it was true one or the other of the two often dipped right or left as Matt leaned against walls or posts. For a change, the whittling knife was safely stashed in a back pocket. Instead Matt Ramsey carried a scribbled list written on the paper cover of a cartridge box.

"I help you?" West asked from behind a counter formed by two planks set atop flour barrels.

Matt studied the trader. Walker West was a smallish man with a balding head and rounded shoulders. His face bore the willing smile common to most merchants and the suspicious eyes painted by years of frontier experience.

"I got a list," Matt muttered, passing the paper to the trader. As West examined the list, Matt gazed around the place. There was just one window, dingy from caked dust and accumulated grime. A coal oil lamp illuminated the place with a kind of smoky yellow glow. On the far side of the trading post two young women examined a barrel of lace cuttings. Near the door a tall black man fingered a coffee tin.

"You got any money?" West asked, tapping the counter. "These things cost, you know. I deal in cash and hides, though I occasionally buy goods I take a likin' to."

"How much?" Matt asked.

West drew out a small tablet and scratched numbers with a pencil. He added them up and circled a total.

"Here," the trader said, turning the tablet so Matt could read it while keeping the paper out of sight from the others.

"It'd seem high," Matt remarked as he drew out the well-worn greenbacks earned supplying remounts to a pair of Wise County ranchers. "I'd judge twenty dollars'd be closer to a fair man's mark."

"Maybe in Jacksboro," West argued. "Not here. I get my price generally."

"I pay what's fair," Matt grumbled, leaving the greenbacks on the counter long enough for West to get a healthy look. "I never took you for the kind to gouge a man in the pocket, mister. Ain't entirely safe to drive a man and his business away, you know."

"Never intended that," West said, shuffling his feet as Matt drew out his whittling knife and cut a slice from the counter. "I guess I can afford to shave my price some for a veteran."

Matt followed the trader's eyes until they fell upon the old brass buckle adorned with an eagle sheltering a single star. Maybe a hundred men from the regiment had bought those buckles down in Houston before beginning the long march to Corinth. It was the only surviving piece of Matt's tattered uniform. Even the leather pistol belt had dissolved last winter.

"Deal?" West asked, extending his small, whitish hand.

"Done," Matt agreed, gripping the hand tightly a second, then letting go.

West took the crumpled banknotes and began gathering the supplies. Matt gazed out the open door to where his eighteen-year-old brother Luke stood waiting with the wagon. It wasn't so long ago Luke was a sandy-haired boy tormenting his older brothers with every manner of prank imaginable. Now Luke was near as tall as Matt, could ride from daybreak to dusk and never show it, and was close to as steady in a fight as Amos or Kyle, the two eldest of the clan. Well, why not? Luke was a Ramsey, too.

"Here you are, fellow," West said, placing a box of supplies atop the counter. Another followed. Matt examined the goods, saw everything was there, and lifted the first box to one shoulder. Three newcomers marched into the store, and Matt deftly dodged them as he carried the box to the wagon. After setting it in back, Matt turned toward the trading post. He was surprised to see the black man appear in the doorway with the second box.

"I believe . . ." Matt began.

"Please, mister," the black mumbled as he headed toward Matt's wagon. The three newcomers marched close behind. Two others approached from the street.

"That your darky?" a dust-covered stranger with long red hair asked.

Matt ignored the question and helped ease the supplies into the wagon.

"I asked you a question!" the redhead barked, grabbing Matt by the arm. The stranger's touch struck a raw nerve, and Matt answered with a heavy right hand that slammed into the red-head's jaw and sent him reeling back into the street.

"You one o' them freedmen's fellows?" a younger man clad in farm overalls asked. "Eh? Like to help 'em out, do you?"

"I got places to be," Matt growled. "Obliged for the help, friend," he added, nodding to the black.

"Sure," the black man answered, turning to face the five drifters alone. "Now, what you want?"

"You," the redhead said, laughing.

"You, mister darky," the young one added. "Always did want to know what it felt like to have my boots polished by a slave."

"I'm nobody's slave," the black replied, angrily doubling his fists. "I'm Lincoln Stokes, and I got as much right here's any-body!"

"Hear that, boys?" the redhead asked. "Lincoln. Well, ole Abe got himself shot, as was fit an' proper for any o' them darky-lovin' Yankees. As for you, Lincoln, we got a rope that needs stretchin'."

Matt saw the supplies packed for the journey to the Trinity, then gave a fretful glance at Luke.

"Matt, no," Luke pleaded. Matt only shrugged his shoulders and stepped down from the wagon.

"Rope stretchin's hard work sometimes," Matt said, edging the farmboy away from Stokes. "How'd you plan to do that?"

"Best way possible," the redhead explained. "With a black neck. Might be we got two ropes to stretch, dependin' on whether some fool with a big nose wants to put it in the middle of my business."

"And if I told you I was makin' it my business?"

"Then we're sure to be at odds, wouldn't you say?"

"So it'd seem," Matt grumbled, turning to Stokes.

"My fight," Stokes insisted.

"Well, I'd never steal a man's property," Matt said, grinning. "I might share it, though."

Stokes lurched forward then, elbowing one man away, block-ing a second to the ground with a powerful shoulder, and driving his head into the belly of a third. The redhead reached for a pistol, but Matt struck first, jabbing three or four times before sending a sledgehammer right into the redhead's nose. The farmboy gazed at Matt's fiery eyes and scrambled off down the street. Lincoln Stokes battered away at two of the stunned drifters while Matt began hammering the third.

Years of anger and resentment exploded inside Matt. Fury gave weight to his fists, and they alternately pummeled one man, then another. The redhead's face swelled purple, and he collapsed. The others, now recovering from shock, struck back.

In a matter of minutes, a crowd gathered. Fancy women shouted encouragement from the roof of a nearby gaming house. A derelict Indian howled. Three seedy buffalo hunters set up a wagering table, but the fight ended before the betting really got going. Stokes exhausted two of them, and Matt sent the last scoundrel crashing into a pile of shoveled horse dung back of the livery.

The crowd cheered Matt and Stokes like heroes. Matt shook the dust from his ragged clothes, gave the redhead a final kick, then wiped blood from a swollen lip.

"Thanks for sharin' your fight," Matt remarked with a crooked smile.

Stokes turned dizzily and answered with a grin. The black man staggered to the wagon, then rested his heavy body against the plank bed.

"You all right?" Matt asked.

"For now," Stokes muttered, nodding to the angry-looking group gathering around the farmboy. "I got to get my horse."

Matt followed Stokes's eyes to where a sorrel pony stood tethered to a hitching post. Luke raced over and brought the horse. Stokes tried to mount, but exhaustion was taking a toll. The big man's shoulders quivered, and he sank to his knees in the dusty street.

"You're comin' with us," Matt insisted.

Stokes started to argue, but he couldn't seem to form the words on his tired lips. Luke tied the sorrel to the wagon, and Matt got Lincoln Stokes up into the bed.

"Where we takin' him?" Luke asked as he slapped the horses into motion.

"Got a home?" Matt asked.

"Got no one," Stokes grumbled. "No one."

"I know the feelin'," Matt muttered, staring eastward toward Fannin County, toward the little farm that had once been home. So much could happen to . . .

Matt tried not to think about it. The ride back to the ranch down on the Trinity would take better than three hours, and it was best spent resting.

Luke kept the wagon rumbling along at a steady pace. Matt dabbed a bit of whiskey on his cuts, then winced as the fiery liquid touched the open wounds. He then doctored Stokes a bit before stretching out in the bed beside the snoring black man. Sleep wouldn't come to Matt Ramsey, though. Instead he found himself staring at the wild grassland coming to life all over again. Grasses and wildflowers promised a better day. That promise, Matt suspected, would not be kept.

Texas, now that the war was over, had become occupied country. Bluecoated soldiers rode in columns across the hills and open range, supposedly sweeping the frontier clear of Indians. More often, the cavalry ran good people off their land as crooked judges grabbed homes from folks who couldn't meet the rising tax bills.

Corn and cotton brought little cash nowadays. There was no way to get goods to market, and scant few markets. Nobody had any cash. The only product of any consequence was Texas beef. Longhorns could carry themselves to Kansas stockyards, and Northern mouths had acquired a taste for steak. But the trail north through the Indian Nations was long and treacherous. Many failed to make it, and others saw their steers stolen within ear-shot of the rails. Still, big trail drives were forming up, and ranchers returning from Wichita with pockets stuffed with green-backs spoke of a new, rich future for the Lone Star State.

Matt remained unconvinced. The Kiowas and Comanches still owned the Llano, and while big ranches spread out from the frontier, many of the little farms were abandoned by threadbare settlers who packed up their wailing women and hollow-cheeked children in hopes of finding better lives elsewhere. Matt Ramsey saw them as the wagon crept southward.

Texas was destitute. Small boys and girls littered the streets of bigger towns, abandoned by parents who had died or simply given up and set out alone. Even Buffalo Springs abounded with them. And, yes, there were the freed slaves.

Matt saw the agony of new freedom etched in Lincoln Stokes's wrinkled brow. There was no freedom from hunger, from the cold, from cruelty and injustice. Back in Fannin County, Matt had returned home one night to witness a good man dangling from a rope—because he'd been born with a black skin. Grown men who never missed Sunday meeting had taken to riding about in sheets, terrorizing . . . sometimes killing.

Death wasn't reserved for freed slaves, though. Matt closed his eyes and recalled the bright eyes of Kate Silcox. She'd grown up in her grandmother's tall house, but that hadn't kept her from wading through the creek with a barechested renegade farmboy named Matt Ramsey. Always, when the turmoil was greatest, Kate had been there to sort it all out. And now she was dead, swept off by a winter chill that stole in like a thief to rob the goodness from life.

"Yes, stole," Matt muttered. It wasn't at all like the death that came from volleys of musket fire or from the tip of a cavalry saber. Death on the battlefield was often as sudden, but somehow it offered a chance to strike back. This other . . .

"You all right, Matt?" Luke called as he slowed the wagon.

"Fine, little brother," Matt answered.

"Little?" Luke complained.

Matt frowned. It wasn't accurate anymore, was it? Luke was a hair short of six-two now, and growing still. He'd been to Kansas and back with their Uncle Russ and had seen three life-time's sorrow in his eighteen winters. Mother and father dead . . . a sister blooming into womanhood swept off by cholera . . . a family rent asunder, sent drifting on the wind like cottonwood seeds, to settle here, there . . . nowhere.

"Look there, Matt," Luke cried, pointing to a pair of bare-chested riders on spotted ponies. "Comanches?"

"No, Kiowas," Matt said, drawing his rifle from beneath the wagon seat and holding it ready. The Indians were mere boys, and their eyes betrayed fear and caution. Matt waved his rifle, and they vanished in the tall grass.

"You figure this country'll ever be altogether tame?" Luke asked. "Even with the new fort down south at Jacksboro, it seems there are Indians about."

"Well, little . . . Luke, this was their country long 'fore it was ours," Matt declared. "As for bein' tame, I'm not sure I'd want it that way. Texas has always been a little raw and trouble-some. Makes her special in a way. No, I wouldn't want her straight-laced and polite. I wouldn't mind her temperin' the weather some, but the cut o' the land suits me well enough."

"I guess if she was too settled, we'd never run down range ponies."

"Be hard, wouldn't it?"

"Amos'll be plantin' back home. Ever miss the farm, Matt?"

"I miss the people," Matt grumbled as he saw their faces. "But they're gone now."

"And the farm? The creek?"

"I remember 'em well enough, Luke, but I was never cut from farmer cloth. That's Amos's way. Me, I been too ready to jump into things, I suppose."

"Like that fight in town?"

"That one and others. You miss the settled ways, Luke?"

"Sure don't miss choppin' cotton," the young man replied, laughing. "I get low sometimes, especially when I get to thinkin' on Ma and Pa. I miss Bucky some, though he's sure one to try your patience with all his pranks and such."

"Range isn't much of a place for a boy of twelve, even if he's a Ramsey."

"Amos sees he stays at his lessons, too. Ma would've taken it hard if Bucky . . . well . . ."

"If he took to the wild ways like Kyle and me?" Matt asked, laughing. "She like to take a stick at me for my penmanship, you know. And figures—well, I was born to run horses and herd cows, Luke."

"And me?"

"You got to find your own road, little brother. But don't hurry yourself. It'll come by and by."

# CHAPTER

## ★ 2 ★

Most of the afternoon had spent itself by the time the wagon rolled along the Trinity River to the twin corrals and plank bunkhouse that made up Matt Ramsey's mustanging headquarters. By that time Lincoln Stokes had returned to life.

"This it?" the weary black man asked when Luke pulled the wagon to a stop.

"Not much of a ranch, eh?" Matt asked. "Well, it's got a roof to keep off the rain, and the corrals hold our horses. No lace curtains or silver teacups."

"Figure I'm used to all that?" Stokes asked.

"You're not?" Matt asked, grinning. "Why, I took you for a manor house dandy, Mr. Stokes."

"Last man called me that was tryin' to sell me a headstone for my ole mama," Stokes answered. "Linc does me better."

"Matt Ramsey," Matt said, extending his hand. "This stringbean of a driver here's my brother Luke."

Linc gripped Matt's hand, then nodded to Luke. Soon three dust-covered men approached from the corral, and Matt introduced the balance of his outfit.

"This is Linc Stokes," Matt explained to the others. He then

9

turned to a crusty buckskin-clad man of forty or so. "Linc, meet Stump Riley. Stump's been runnin' down range ponies since the sun first crossed the sky. He's a pitiful poor excuse for a cook, and he snores bad as you do, but he plays a fair fiddle and chases off some of the melancholy."

Linc held out his hand, but Riley only eyed the newcomer with suspicion.

"Don't let it worry you much," the younger of two yellow-haired young men said as he gripped Linc's hand. "Stump takes some gettin' used to."

"Not half as much as you, Peewee," Riley countered. " 'Round here a man's apt to find himself tyin' diapers, what with all these babes and all Matt's signed on."

"Least we haven't gone bald and bowlegged," the youngster replied, grinning.

"Might as well know straight out, Linc," Matt said, shaking his head. "When I brought Luke along, I got myself saddled with Eli here, too. Eli Lyttel, Linc. This other fellow back here, the quiet one, calls himself Gil Coleridge. He used to chase my kid sister around, and I guess he's kind of taken to followin' me into whatever foolishness comes to my addled mind."

"Glad to meet you, Linc," Gil said, shaking the newcomer's hand.

"So what is it you do with yourselves out here?" Linc asked.

"Mostly we run down range horses," Matt explained.

"Mostly we talk 'bout it," Stump objected. "I ain't seen that much real work goin' on."

"We brought in a dozen mustangs back in February," Matt said, frowning in Riley's direction. "Delivered the last one three days back. Now it's time to set off after some more."

"I thank you for what you did in town," Linc said, "but truth is, I never done much work with horses."

"Got those shoulders liftin' hay, did you?" Matt asked. "That how your hands got burn scarred? You've been a blacksmith. The work's marked you. We could use a man who can hammer out shoes, shape bridles and bits, help some with the horses."

"I didn't make many friends in town. Better I head on."

"To where?" Matt asked. "Here we share equal what's left once supplies are bought. Won't make you rich, but then you won't have to keep lookin' over your shoulder to see who's chasin' you."

"I got no tools," Linc complained. "I'd need things."

"We'll get 'em," Matt promised. "Can you shoot?"

"Try me," Linc said grimly. "Bring that redheaded fellow by. I'll bet I hit the bullseye every time."

Matt laughed, then told the others about the set-to in Buffalo Springs.

"You watch he doesn't get you in a worse fix 'fore he's through," Eli warned. "Matt's got a nose for findin' a fight. Close to the best at it I ever saw."

"I've also got a nose for smellin' rank wranglers," Matt added, lifting Eli off his feet and carrying him to the river. The protesting youngster kicked his feet and flailed his arms, all to no avail. Matt pitched the eighteen-year-old into the river and turned, howling, to face Luke.

"I learned a long time ago it was better to go in on my own," Luke said, kicking off his boots, shedding his sweat-soaked shirt, and discarding what remained en route to the river. Gil followed.

"Stump?" Matt called to the old-timer.

"Bath's not healthy for a man o' my years," Stump argued.

"Indians live forever, 'less some fool shoots 'em," Matt answered. "Never saw a cleaner people than the Kiowas who camp 'round here."

"Comin'?" Linc asked, stretching to his full six and a half feet. "I kind o' got a likin' for tossin' ole white folks 'round, you know."

Stump muttered to himself and trudged along to the river. Matt swapped grins with Linc, then shook off his clothes and stepped into the refreshing waters. The river seemed to wash away worries and weariness as it removed dust and sweat and grime. Luke and Eli were soon romping about splashing and wrestling anyone who didn't step clear. When they reached Linc, they froze.

Matt, too, saw the scars.

"Left by a white man's lash," Linc explained. "Plantation medicine, he called it, for them that didn't step lively. Got the first strokes when I was fourteen. The last just 'fore we got word o' th' emancipation."

"Never had a lot o' dealin's with slaves," Luke said, sitting beside Linc in the shallows. "Was it hard bein' a slave?"

"Sometimes," Linc confessed. "Sometimes it's just hard bein' alive."

"Or stayin' that way," Eli added. "They hung my pa, you know. Was on account they said we were hidin' a wagon we weren't supposed to have. Mainly it was 'cause Pa spoke against the war."

"Oh?" Linc asked as Eli's smile gave way to a bitter scowl.

"Ole Jeremiah, one o' the Silcox hands, used to talk to me 'bout the slave days," Luke said sourly. "That was after the war was over. He said hardest part was not havin' family. I'd guess it so. Ma and Pa are gone three, four years now, and I feel it still."

"I had a family," Linc said, grinning as he stared southward across the river. "Silvy, that was my lady's name. As pure pretty as a midnight sky, with eyes like stars on Easter mornin'. Oh, we had some fine plans, we did."

"You goin' to meet her someplace?" Gil asked.

"The Lord called her away," Linc whispered. "She's singin' glory hymns with the angels now, she and the little one who couldn't get himself born. Hard losin' a woman that way, right in her hour o' glory."

"It's never easy," Gil declared. "Cholera took Anna Louise, Matt and Luke's sister. Always figured we'd be married when I got my growth. Well, here I am twenty now, and she's dead three years. How do you figure that?"

"You don't," Linc grumbled as he splashed back to the bank.

For a time the big smith sat beneath a swaying willow, frowning and staring into the distance. Then he got into his clothes and set about tending his horse. Stump didn't linger a second longer. Soon he was shouting for Luke and Eli to help unload the supplies, and the two eighteen-year-olds scrambled up the bank as well.

Gil and Matt stayed in the creek a bit longer.

"Still grievin' for her after all this time?" Matt asked.

"Can't help myself," Gil explained. "Never knew anybody else like Anna Louise."

"Seems to me it's time we got you to town more then," Matt remarked. "Can't have you wastin' away the best years of your life out there with a bunch o' range ponies."

"Think I ought to share myself with the rest o' womankind, huh?"

"It's a thought, Gil," Matt said, laughing at his young friend. "A thought."

"You're not so old yourself, Matt," Gil added as they left the river. "Bit scarred up, but you've still got your teeth."

"I'm not but twenty-five!" Matt cried. "Not time to bury me for a few weeks yet."

"Well, it's you talks like you're old and gray," Gil complained. "Maybe we ought to ride down to Jacksboro, see if they plan another one o' those barn dances."

"Bad idea!" Luke called from the wagon. "Matt like to take on half the Sixth Cavalry at the last one, all on account they made some remarks about Texans stealin' boots off Union dead at Shiloh."

"Called us buzzards," Matt said, grinding his teeth. "That ugly fool of a corporal's lucky I only cracked one o' his ribs."

"You were lucky he couldn't reach that pistol," Luke added. "He'd have shot you dead, Matt. No, I think you'd best stay clear o' Jacksboro for a bit yet."

"Guess we'll have to leave the gals to Gil's charms then."

"There's plenty to go 'round," Gil claimed, combing the thin hairs of his moustache into place. "Plenty."

"Most words I heard that boy speak since I known him," Matt said, laughing.

Once supplies were stashed in the larder and the horses were cared for, Stump started a stew to boiling. Matt collected the youngsters at the empty corral. They sat on the top rail and watched a pair of ducks settle on the surface of the river.

"Want I should fetch a rifle?" Luke whispered.

"We got food for tonight," Matt said, taking out his knife and whittling on an oak limb. "Just leave 'em be. They're pretty to watch."

"Are at that," Luke admitted. "I always did think ducks and geese had a special way o' puttin' people at ease. Cy Liberty called 'em angel birds. He said they come o' heaven, though I got to admit no goose I ever heard sounded like a choir."

"No, indeed," Linc agreed, joining Matt and the youngsters. "Who you say told you 'bout those birds, Luke?"

"Cyrus Liberty," Luke explained. "After Ma and Pa died, Cy and his brother came to our place to help work the land."

"He was like me, a black man?" Linc asked.

"Yeah," Luke muttered. "Good man, Cy. Worked hard, but he never seemed to mind. His hands made the land bloom."

"I recall meetin' a fellow called himself Liberty," Linc said, nodding. "That was at a place east o' here callin' itself Lincolntown."

"Might've been Cy," Matt said. "Fannin County? Our farm was out that way."

"Lost my boy in a fire there," Linc said, resting his chin in his hands. "This Liberty and another man helped pull l'il Toby from the fire, but he swallowed too much smoke. Boy was never strong after Silvy left us."

"You lost a boy, too?" Matt asked.

"Whatever come o' that Liberty?" Linc asked.

"Some fellows hung him," Luke whispered.

"Same ones that hung Pa, 'cept they were masked when they lynched Cy," Eli added.

"Those were hard days," Matt grumbled.

"You seen some of 'em, have you?" Linc asked, gazing into Matt's eyes.

"My share, I suppose," Matt replied.

"Got a deep hurt in there someplace," Linc said. "I seen it in my own face after Silvy . . . after she died."

"Her name was Kate," Matt whispered. Luke gripped his brother's shivering right shoulder. Eli and Gil gazed in a kind of reverent silence.

"A wife?" Linc asked.

"Would've been, I think," Matt continued. "Though why she'd hitch herself to the likes of me, I'll never know. She was too fine by half to put up with such faults as I've stacked up over the years. She had a gentleness to her touch, and she understood when I needed a little patience. Underneath there was a hardness that made her strong. Only woman I ever took to my heart."

"She died of a fever," Luke explained. "Hit real sudden. Doc hadn't even been called."

"No reason to," Matt explained. "She never took ill more'n a day or two in all her life. I saw it in the war, though, how a soldier could fight his way across a dozen battlefields, then cough out his life o' camp fever."

"My ole mama used to say the Lord brings a man troubles to make him strong," Linc said, nodding respectfully.

"Pa thought so," Matt recalled, cutting a sizable slice from the oak limb. "He's dead, though. Sometimes it seems the Lord only brings a man hard times to make him dead."

"I suppose it'd seem so," Linc confessed. "But I like to think it's how Mama thought. There's comfort in the notion. I like to think o' my Silvy and your Kate singin' with the angels, Matt."

"Kate sang like a frog," Matt said, laughing as he recalled the time she'd broken out in a whiskey-inspired rendition of "Dixie" when her grandmother had invited the new federal occupation garrison commander to dinner.

"She did," Luke agreed. "But maybe up there all that changes."

"Could be," Linc agreed.

Stump then shouted that supper was ready, and the hungry outfit charged toward the bunkhouse. There would be time for sharing melancholy tales later. Now was the time to fill bellies and chase away gloom.

After supper, Matt and Luke scrubbed the plates clean while Stump tuned his fiddle. It wasn't long before jaunty tunes floated across the darkening landscape, and the mustangers joined in bawdy ballads and old camp songs. Linc added a new one, a somber spiritual that suited his deep bass voice better than the high tenor notes of Luke and Eli.

"That was fine indeed," Matt commented as he put away the last dried platter and led Luke outside. "Know another?"

Linc knew a dozen, and in time the others picked up the words. Stump even managed to fiddle something similar to the melody, and the singing lasted well after the sun did.

When yawns finally overwhelmed voices, the weary mustangers took to their blankets. Linc drew Matt aside. With sorrowful eyes, the big blacksmith said, "I owe you my life, Matt Ramsey."

"No such thing," Matt argued. "They'd never really hang you. Even if they'd tried, you were close to a fair match for the lot of 'em."

"Wasn't talkin' 'bout the fight," Linc explained. "You brought my soul back from the darkness. I'd give up, you see. Was talkin' 'bout Silvy and the boys, or maybe listenin' to them boys and all their sadnesses. Or maybe it was the bath."

"I feel older'n hell bein' 'round this bunch," Matt confessed. "Luke, why, he's just seven years short o' bein' my age, but he's more son than brother. Same with Eli and Gil. Kind o' nice to have another grown man 'round, Linc."

"I'll see you're not sorry to've brought me along. I pay my debts, you know."

"Nothin's owed," Matt declared. "Nothin' at all, Linc. Now you're here, you're a partner like everybody else. You share in the work and the profits."

"Then I guess we'd best find some to share."

"Would seem a fair notion," Matt admitted.

# CHAPTER

## ★ 3 ★

Early the following morning, Matt Ramsey roused his companions from a heavy slumber and set them about making ready for a fortnight on the plains. Sometimes it took days to even locate sign of range ponies. Then, like as not, the unshod hooves proved to belong to a Kiowa hunting party.

Horses needed water, though, and the shallow draws and box canyons along the Trinity were the likeliest hiding places for the elusive mustangs. Boxed in by steep banks, the horses offered more cooperative targets for a wrangler's rope than when running free across the range.

Twice before Matt had led his young companions into the spotted hills north of the Trinity. There, where not long ago herds of buffalo grazed, stray longhorns escaped from trail drives crowded the creekbeds and river bottoms. Those prowling cattle provided the mustangers with food to fill empty bellies and hides that could be worked into lariats or clothing.

"If a man has eyes to find it, the land will provide what he needs," old Sam Ramsey had taught his sons. Matt had learned the lesson well. He kept his crew content by pitching camp near sheltered springs and by keeping fresh meat in the stewpot.

It was horses, though, that would put silver in their pockets. And with the ranches driving thousands of longhorns to market in Kansas, with stage relays and Yank cavalry needing stock, and with Kiowa and Comanche raiders stealing any animal they could, there was a constant shortage of saddle mounts. Even though a mustang wasn't as pretty to gaze at, it was the kind of horse that would carry a man through thunder and back.

The first task ahead of the mustangers was spotting their quarry. Range ponies ran free because they'd learned to stay well clear of the ranches and farms that marked the edge of white settlement. More difficult was avoiding the favored camping grounds of the Indians. Most bands followed a leader—some fierce, strong-willed stallion as swift and cunning as any cavalry general. Abandoned war ponies or remounts escaped from a remuda often joined these bands, swelling their ranks even as outfits like Matt's did their best to whittle them down.

Some mustangers set off to take the lead stallion and bring the other animals along later. Matt preferred to take the refugee ranch horses and the stallions that raced along the flanks of the herd. No lead stallion would ever really take the bit, and left to his own instincts, those stallions would rebuild their bands in a single summer.

Matt was prone to roping colts. They were easier to bend to human will, and if a buyer wanted geldings, that was best done with the very young. Of course, a colt wanted time to grow, and it would be a while before the pony was ready to carry a man. So Matt took care not to overburden his outfit with young stock.

Ten miles from the bunkhouse, Matt split his crew into pairs. "Anybody spots a trail, send a man back here. We'll meet at noon, eat somethin', then head out again if nobody finds anything."

"We know what's to be done," Luke answered. Then he and Eli set off westward along the river. Matt sent Linc Stokes with a reluctant Stump Riley into the northern hills.

"Guess that leaves us, eh, Matt?" Gil asked, turning his horse toward the northwest.

"I've kept worse company," Matt said, leading the way.

For most of that morning Matt scoured the range for traces of mustangs. But in the end, it was Gil who spotted the pony trail. Matt cautiously followed as Gil led the way down a shallow ravine. At the far end, a midnight black stallion led a collection of some forty animals toward the Trinity.

"Fetch the others," Matt whispered. "You done fine, Gil."

Gil nodded, then began working his way back up the ravine toward the rendezvous spot.

Another man might have felt nervous, stalking the herd alone. Matt was at ease. He'd ridden alone often, and he was on familiar ground. The horses posed no real danger. At worst they would pick up the scent of a stranger and stampede into the hills. Though that would make his job harder, Matt knew in the end his crew would round up enough ponies to keep them busy for a time.

While he awaited the others, Matt chewed some jerked beef and took note of which animals seemed soundest of limb. The big black would be left to run free as would the lead mares. Matt and Stump would charge the center, breaking off the rear batch from their companions. Then it would merely be a matter of roping and corraling the captive horses.

It was toward mid-afternoon when the rest of the mustangers joined Matt in the ravine. By that time the herd had moved down to a creek lined by treacherous sandstone walls. Another thirty horses had joined the fierce black, and others continued to swell the herd.

"I never seen so many horses," Linc declared. "We can't grab all of 'em."

"No," Matt agreed. But as he eyed the animals, he envisioned a plan whereby perhaps forty or fifty might be held. He immediately explained his plan, and the mustangers set to work erecting a rock wall across the ravine's eastern exit. Then, each of them soaked with sweat and weary from the effort, the outfit cut around the herd and started down the steep embankment toward the horses.

The big black instantly took note of the crumbling rock. He turned his nose to the air, sniffing out the scent of men carried by a quiet breeze. Snorting and stomping, the stallion urged its mares along as it headed eastward from the danger.

Matt waved the others along as he charged toward the fleeing animals, howling and slapping his hat against his knee. The animals turned and raced into the trap.

"Hurry now," Matt urged as he pulled up short. Eli and Luke tied off their horses and began felling trees to block the western

exit. If the black didn't tumble to the plan, the whole herd would
be trapped in a perfect high-walled corral. The stallion wasn't
one to be penned up, though. Even as the wall of oak and rock
rose higher, the big ebony stallion was fighting his way up a
gully to safety. Three of the mares and a half-dozen stallions
also managed to escape. The others failed. They remained in
the natural corral, awaiting the ropes that would lead them into
captivity.

Matt couldn't help gazing at the horses atop the embankment
as they stared down at their helpless companions. Mares whinnied at their young. Stallions reared up on hind legs, seemingly
fighting the air that separated their mates. Then, defeated, the
big black led away the remaining free horses while Matt prepared to deal with the mass of stomping animals trapped in the
ravine.

For more than a week Matt and his companions busied themselves cutting out weaned colts and fillies from the herd, then
dragging them back to the work corrals at the Trinity. Stump
and Linc remained there, guarding the wild ponies and erecting
a third, larger corral for the captured animals. In all, forty-seven
mustangs were brought in. A handful escaped the confines of
the ravine, and two broke loose en route and scrambled to freedom. Even so, it was a record haul, and Matt celebrated by
tossing his hat in the air and uncorking a bottle of Jack County
corn.

The liquor drove them into an early deep sleep, and they
greeted the morning with ringing ears. There would be no joy
thereafter. Too much work lay ahead of them.

The mustangs, even the sleek ones with proud heads and swift
feet, would fetch no price raw and rebellious as they were. The
challenge facing Matt Ramsey was to bend the fierce will of the
mustang so that its spirit could be harnessed. Matt had merely
to gaze at the first colt to recall the aches in his hips and back
left from being tossed about or slammed against a corral rail.
Nevertheless, he roped the first stallion and led the beast to the
work corral.

Stump waited, branding iron in hand. Gil and Eli slung loops
over the stormy animal's head, and Matt forced the horse down
so that Stump could add the Circle R brand worn by the livestock
of Matt's Uncle Russ down south. Then it was time for the next
animal. All day, and on into the fading light of dusk, the brand-

ing went on. Linc busied himself gelding the colts, all save the more handsome Matt thought held value as breeders. In the heat and dust, amid whining horses that stomped and bit, the tempers of the men flared. Only the afternoon swims kept them from igniting.

"This outfit needs a rest," Stump told Matt after Luke and Eli engaged in a furious fistfight over which one had swallowed the most dust.

"I know," Matt confessed. "But it won't be long before the ranchers are ready to buy stock for their trail crews, and none of these ponies is fit for market yet."

So Matt set his weary and testy companions to work gentling range ponies, exchanging their stubborn wildness for strength and compliance. If there was a harder task on earth, Matt had never seen it.

By and by the horses took the bit, allowed first saddle and then rider on their backs. Linc managed to hammer out iron shoes for their hooves. By mid-April Matt had twenty-three horses ready to market.

The first buyers were ranchers. They held their purses tightly, and they bid under the value of every horse in the corral.

"You won't do better elsewhere," a tall man named Fretz declared. "Twenty dollars is a top price."

"For a yearling colt maybe," Matt argued. "I want fifty for that roan stallion, and the white mare's forty-five. If I can't sell 'em at that, I'll breed 'em and start my own string. Good horses, those."

Before the month was out, Matt sold fifteen of the better horses, most at near his price. Then word came that a federal agent would visit the horse ranches to purchase twenty cavalry remounts.

"Twenty?" Stump asked excitedly. "That'd about be all we got ready. You may want to hold onto the rest, especially those spry fillies and the two nutmeg colts. They'd build you a fine string, Matt."

"Sure would," Luke readily agreed. "Won't be range ponies out there forever, you know. Sooner or later we'll have to breed our own."

"Sure," Matt admitted. How could he explain a reluctance to set down roots, to tie himself to a ranchhouse when Eli and Luke swapped treasured memories of home nightly?

The federal buyers arrived shortly thereafter. There were three of them, squat fellows in a carriage who resembled Ohio bankers more than horse buyers. In truth, Matt doubted a one of them had sat atop a saddle for more than an hour in ten years or more.

Accompanying the buyers was Captain George Washburn of Company C, Sixth U. S. Cavalry. The captain wore the eagles of a brevet colonel on his shoulders, and he rode with an air of arrogance Matt had left behind in Mississippi.

"So, this is your stock, is it?" the captain began as the buyers climbed down from their carriage. "Not much to look at, I fear. Your name's Randolph?"

"Ramsey," Matt said sourly. "Matt Ramsey. That's my brother Luke and Eli Lyttel at the corral gate there. This one here beside me's Gil Coleridge. Gil, I'll bet these fellows could do with a sip o' mint tea."

Gil turned toward the buyers. They nodded, and Gil set off to fetch the tea.

"Your men are likely tired," Matt told Washburn. "Why don't you have them water their horses down at the river. I'll bet we can scare up some food for 'em."

"They have their rations!" the officer responded angrily. "You can rely on me to see to their welfare."

"I'll do just that," Matt said, staring hard at the cavalry commander. "Guess I'd better show my horses."

While Gil offered mugs of tea to the buyers, Matt had Luke and Eli bring out the horses for a closer look. The buyers seemed reluctant to examine the animals. Instead, Washburn and a pair of cavalry sergeants climbed up and put the horses through their paces.

"Seem lively enough," Washburn pronounced.

"Sure-footed," a sergeant named Calvin declared. "Better'n what we've been gettin' by a long shot."

"Well, then perhaps we can have something to eat and discuss price," the chief buyer, Patrick Spander, suggested.

"We've got some cold beef and biscuits, if that'd suit you," Gil said.

"And I've brought along a bottle of peach brandy to seal the bargain," Spander replied. "Well, friends, shall we carry on?"

Gil set off to cut slices of beef and locate the biscuits. Matt helped the soldiers tie up the horses, then showed them a suitable place to shade themselves from the midday heat.

Washburn stayed up the hill with the buyers. Sergeant Calvin started to issue rations, but Matt shook his head at the sight of tinned beans and salted bacon.

"There's plenty o' fresh beef for all, sergeant," Matt whispered. "If you think we might be able to get it smuggled past that bunch o' brass buttons yonder."

"Ramsey, I smuggled tobacco past the nose of Ulysses S. Grant at Vicksburg," Calvin said, grinning. "Lead away."

In no time at all Matt had two rump roasts and a sack of bread headed toward the river encampment of the soldiers. The men were a mixture of bearded veterans of the war and stubble-cheeked youngsters recruited from every jailhouse and river landing north of the Ohio River. Some were foreigners, eager to take any job that promised a full belly and an occasional nip of whiskey.

"Not much like my last regiment," Calvin grumbled. "Lot o' fine boys in that outfit. Got themselves killed, most of 'em, but you never worried they'd run off in the night."

The half-dozen veterans gathered together and recalled the hard months campaigning on the Mississippi.

"We won the war when we took Vicksburg, you know," one declared. "Now nobody even remembers the place."

"I do," Matt said, staring off toward the east. "I was there."

"Oh?" Sergeant Calvin asked. "Officer?"

"Me?" Matt asked, laughing. "I was too fond o' foragin' and too smart by half for that. Wore corporal's stripes toward the end. That's as military as they could ever persuade me to be."

"I wore captain's bars the last year," Calvin explained. "But to be a real brass bottom, you need a senator for an uncle."

"Like Washburn," one of the privates said, grinning. "Fool couldn't fight his way out of a fancy house."

"By the cut of him, he wouldn't be much use inside one, either," another soldier said, laughing. "So far he's kept busy with this and that, leavin' us to chase Indians."

"That's why you don't see any arrows stickin' out of us," Calvin declared.

"Sergeant!" Washburn suddenly hollered from the top of the hill.

"Guess it's time to rejoin the army," Calvin said, setting his food aside for the moment. "Anyhow, thanks for the beef, Ramsey. Maybe we can return the favor someday."

"Maybe," Matt said, nodding as the sergeant raced to his commander's side.

Matt remained behind for a few minutes, swapping remembrances with the soldiers. Then Luke trotted over and asked him to return to the corral.

"They're ready to buy, Matt," the younger Ramsey declared. "Lord, they've got a whole bag full o' money. I'll bet we do just fine on this deal."

Matt hoped so. He followed Luke back to where the buyers stood chatting with Washburn and Calvin.

"You seem on good terms with our men," Spander observed.

"Old comrades, so to speak," Matt explained.

Sergeant Calvin seemed a bit uncomfortable, but Matt only smiled.

"We were talkin' about the Vicksburg campaign," Matt went on to say. "Not that I know all that much, bein' no more'n a corporal when we surrendered."

"You took up arms with the rebs?" Washburn asked.

"Most hereabouts did," Matt answered. "I'm not particular proud of it, but I'm not ashamed, either."

"Maybe you should be," Washburn suggested. "Bunch of murderin' scum, you rebels. Mr. Spander, I'm afraid we won't be able to make this transaction after all. My uncle, the senator, was quite clear as to his views on buying stock from rebels."

"War's over, George," Spander argued. "We need horses."

"Over?" Washburn asked icily. "Tell that to my brother Hiram who fell at Gettysburg. Tell it to young Jeff, who was just seventeen when that devil Forrest blew him up at Johnsonville!"

"We've all of us suffered losses," Matt said coldly. "Pain doesn't fade with a few scratches on a paper. Now we're on the same side, though. You need horses to keep the peace, to patrol the prairie. I got some to sell."

"Not to us," Washburn insisted.

"Fine," Matt barked. "Go back to Jacksboro and buy those nags your carpetbagger friends'll sell you. Check the brokers in Millstown. They'll rob you and sell you mounts that'll give way the first hard ride they take. I've got good stock. Horses can always be sold in Texas. You'll be the one to be sorry, captain."

"It's colonel!" Washburn growled.

"Whatever it is, you wait just a minute," Linc protested, charging out the bunkhouse door. In seconds he stood towering over Washburn, glaring at the bluecoat's eyes. "You can believe I didn't take up no arms agin' the Union. My hands shoed these horses, roped 'em and broke 'em to saddle. Those boys yonder weren't old enough to soldier. Why not think this over a bit?"

"He's right," Spander said, gripping Washburn's arm.

"So now you'd buy from *him*?" Washburn cried. "You must've lost your mind. I don't bargain with traitors or . . . Well, I'd prefer not to favor that one with a reply."

Washburn then executed a precise turn and marched to his horse. Sergeant Calvin extended Matt a look of sympathy, then set about getting his command organized.

Fifteen minutes later, the buyers and their cavalry escorts were headed eastward toward Millstown.

"Well, friends," Matt lamented, "I guess it wasn't to be."

"No," Linc grumbled. "Would've been too easy. Lord never made me a smooth path in all my years."

"Nor the rest of us, either," Matt said, sitting and staring at the surging waters of the Trinity. "More ranchers'll be around to buy soon. We'll sell 'em all right."

"Sure," Luke agreed.

But in truth little confidence greeted those words.

# CHAPTER

## ★ 4 ★

As the nearby cattle ranches began collecting longhorns and preparing for the long trek up the Chisholm Trail to Kansas, Matt and his companions appeared with their horses. A rancher would purchase a pinto mare in the morning. That afternoon a freighter might take on a pair of stallions. Sometimes Eli or Luke would sell a saddle pony to a travelling preacher. So it was that the corrals began to empty. And if prices failed to measure up to Matt's expectations, well, any cash money at all was a blessing on the penniless frontier.

It was while delivering a pair of geldings to a Millstown baker that Luke and Eli spotted a small herd of mustangs not more than five miles from the bunkhouse. Eli continued into town with the ponies while Luke galloped back to fetch Matt and the others.

"How many were there?" Matt asked as he steadied his breathless brother.

"Fifteen or twenty," Luke said between gasps. "Just grazin' on buffalo grass calm as you please. We could grab 'em and be back in an hour, Matt."

When Eli rode in an hour later with much the same story, Matt began saddling his horse.

"Linc, you stay with Stump and watch the place," Matt said. He thought to leave Gil, too, but upon gazing at the excited face of the twenty-year-old, Matt knew better. Besides, it would likely take the four of them to round up the mustangs and bring them in.

As they rode out across the empty hillsides beyond the river, Eli and Luke jabbered away about the horses. Gil, as usual, said little. Matt scanned the far horizon for trouble.

"Whenever a thing appears too easy, give her a long, hard look, son," Sam Ramsey had taught his boys. Matt took such wisdom to heart. He felt strangely uneasy about those horses, and he'd taken the precaution of tying his big-bore Sharps behind his saddle.

"Don't mean to shoot any buffalo, do you?" Luke had asked.

"Maybe ought to shoot little brothers with mouths too big for their own good," Matt had answered.

But when the horses appeared just as Luke had described, even Matt agreed their capture proved a simple matter.

Actually, Luke and Eli did most of the work. They charged the grazing mustangs with rare fury, shouting and slapping rope ends at the startled ponies. Then Matt and Gil turned the herd toward the Trinity. For several minutes, the little horses gave their tormentors a real run of it. Then, chests afire from breathing dust, the horses slowed. Matt had little difficulty turning them down a dry creekbed that led toward the river.

The trouble started shortly thereafter. At first Matt only sensed the other riders. He felt they were there, but his eyes detected nothing. Then a bronze face gazed out from between two black locust trees, and a single, barrel-chested horseman appeared ahead, seemingly blocking the creekbed with his intense stare.

"Hold up the horses," Matt called.

Luke and Eli pinched the lead animals until the mustangs came to a halt. Then the young mustangers froze.

"Matt, Kiowas," Luke announced.

Immediately half a dozen Indians joined their dour-faced leader.

"Look at that scar across his face," Luke called to Matt.

"Yes," Matt muttered. A knife or a saber had closed one of

the Indian's eyes, leaving a single white orb to watch the approaching riders.

"It's One Eye," Luke announced. "I heard of him, Matt. They say he's torched half the frontier. One minute he's burnin' stage depots at Jacksboro. The next he's raidin' ranches over in Wise County."

Matt had heard the stories, too. They hadn't concerned him much. After all, frontier tales had a way of growing with each telling. Now One Eye was here, blocking Matt's trail, bringing danger to himself and his companions.

"I've heard he's scalped twenty men," Eli said, nervously nudging his horse back toward Matt. "Some women and kids, too. Peeled off all their skin and left 'em for their folks to find."

"Oh, he'd never do that to you, Eli," Matt assured the youngster. "Likely just shoot you once or twice."

"That'd be enough," Eli said with alarm. "What do we do, Matt?"

Luke and Gil gazed with equal concern toward their leader. Matt loosened the rawhide strips holding the Sharps in place and drew the rifle from its resting place. Instantly One Eye raised his arm, and the Kiowas surged forward.

"Turn the horses!" Matt ordered as he galloped up the slope. Then he swung the Sharps toward the attacking Kiowas and fired the first shot. The Sharps's heavy projectile slammed into a young Kiowa's side, and the boy fell from his saddle. As Matt reloaded, Gil opened fire with a pistol. A second Indian collapsed in his saddle. The others, shaken by their enemy's fire, drew back toward One Eye.

The shots sent the mustangs into a wild stampede. Matt gazed helplessly as half the herd broke free and raced off onto the plain. Eli and Luke managed to contain a dozen or so and coax them into a small ravine.

"So what now?" Gil called as One Eye rallied his raiders.

"Back in the draw," Matt said, turning toward the horses and waving Gil along.

The Kiowas were still recovering from their retreat when Matt reached Luke. The two brothers exchanged nervous, exhausted glances. Then Matt coughed the dust from his lungs and examined the terrain.

"We'll never hold the horses here," Matt said, frowning.

"Luke, you and Eli figure you can drive this batch back to the corrals?"

"Easier'n you can hold off those Indians," Eli answered. "Better we should stick together."

"Gil, maybe you should . . ." Matt began.

"I'm not much good runnin' from a fight," Gil objected. "I do just fine firin' this rifle from cover, though."

"Go, Luke," Matt ordered, gazing intently into his brother's eyes. "When you get the horses tended, tell Linc and Stump what's happened. Like as not we'll wind up leadin' these Kiowas right back to you. Best be ready."

"We will be," Luke promised, swallowing hard. Eli nodded his understanding as well. Then Luke started nudging the mustangs up the ravine and on toward the Trinity.

"So, how do we do it, Matt?" Gil asked.

"Tie your horse to that willow," Matt suggested, dismounting and securing his own animal to a nearby live oak. "Then let's find ourselves a good spot to hold. If we're lucky, they'll grow tired o' losin' men and give it up."

"And if we're not lucky?"

"You never planned to live forever, did you?"

"Guess not," Gil grumbled as Matt led the way into a pile of boulders.

One Eye was a while coming. Matt anchored his Sharps and positioned Gil five feet away. They both expected the Kiowas to come charging up the hill on horseback and overrun them. The Kiowas would pay a cost, of course, but there was really no way of stopping them.

One Eye wasn't one to squander men, however. There was no wild charge. Instead the Kiowas crept toward the ravine in pairs, one shooting an arrow while the other moved forward. It worked well, since every time Matt prepared to shoot, an arrow caused him to leap back.

*You're a crafty devil, all right,* Matt thought. *Come on, One Eye, let's settle this.*

The first figure to fill Matt's sights wasn't the Kiowa leader, though. Instead a boy of perhaps thirteen, naked but for a bit of blanket wrapped around his waist, rushed toward the rocks. Matt drew his revolver and shot the youngster through the left leg. The boy yelped in pain and rolled over behind the safety of a clump of yucca.

"I'd stay put, boys!" Matt called. "You've got more courage than good sense. Next one up I'll be killin'."

The Kiowas replied in a torrent of phrases Matt didn't understand. One half-grown Kiowa stood up and bared himself in defiance. Gil fired, and the boy fell.

It was One Eye's turn to howl angrily. Matt watched as the scarred warrior checked on his wounded companions, then hurled insults at the two whites holding the hill.

"Howl at the wind for all the good it does!" Matt countered. They were so alike, Matt and that Indian! There they stood, old warriors chasing shadows, leading bands of children who had no notion of real fighting . . . or dying.

*How's it possible?* Matt wondered. At twenty-five he was already a frequent visitor to death's door. He felt older, looked older. Yes, the war and its aftermath had left Matt Ramsey wrinkled with worry and scarred by experience.

"Here they come," Gil called.

Matt watched four Indians rise and unleash arrows. Three youngsters hurled themselves toward the rocks. The Sharps barked, and the first one spun like a top before falling. Gil fired, too, rapidly and without aiming. The shot went wide. Matt grabbed the heavy Sharps and leaped out into the open, clubbing one raider to the ground and felling the second with a hard jab in the ribs.

Then, as suddenly as the Kiowas had appeared, they vanished. One Eye chanted loudly, and the Indians left their positions and scrambled back to find their horses.

"Guess God's got a sense of humor," Gil observed. "Gets us ready to face Him, then grants us mercy. Lord, they were close, Matt. I do believe I could feel one of 'em breathin' on me!"

Matt didn't respond. Instead he reloaded his pistol and watched One Eye ride defiantly closer. The Indian sent verbal daggers through the air. Although Matt understood none of the words, it wasn't hard to guess their meaning. One Eye rode away reluctantly, and Matt knew the Kiowas would call again.

Matt and Gil arrived at the bunkhouse just as Stump was ladling beef stew into four wooden bowls.

"Lord, Matt, you're here after all!" Luke shouted as he pulled his brother off the horse. "Are they chasin' you?"

"Not as I saw," Matt said, glancing behind him. "I figure they've got some mendin' to do first."

"Does seem likely," old Stump agreed. "Once they get a sniff o' this place, though, they're apt to be around."

Matt nodded sadly, then shoved his brother along toward the kitchen table. Two more bowls of stew were made ready, and the whole outfit joined in a fretful supper.

"Get back with the horses all right?" Matt finally asked.

"Save one," Luke answered. "Eleven in all, but two of those are branded. Likely Indians run 'em off from cattle drives."

"I'll send word to the owners," Matt pledged.

Eli then started clearing the table while Luke and Gil began scrubbing the stew bowls. Linc took over the watch, allowing old Stump a needed rest.

On toward nightfall, Matt heard something splash into the river. He grabbed the Sharps and trotted out to investigate, but it proved to be a pair of longhorns enjoying a drink.

"Indians come quiet, like shadows," Linc said, joining Matt at the bank. "Nothin' so silent as a prowlin' Comanche."

"They won't come here," Matt said, gazing at the dying sun. "Wasn't but a bunch o' kids followin' that One Eye."

"Same batch's been settin' half the countryside afire," Linc argued. "They could come."

"We shot 'em up some, and that was out in the open, with horses to watch. Here, with the bunkhouse for cover and the river blockin' the approach from the south, they'd pay a high price. I saw that Indian's face when the first boy fell. One Eye's got no stomach to bury anybody else."

"And you?"

"Well, we're alike that way, I guess," Matt said, sitting beneath a willow and taking out his whittling knife. For a bit he and Linc sat there together in the fading light. Then Gil came along. Finally Luke and Eli appeared.

"It was a close thing today," Luke said, settling in beside his brother's feet. "You done lots o' shootin' at folks, Matt. And had 'em after you, too. Me, I never was in such a tough spot before."

"Wasn't much to it," Matt said. "They didn't press it."

"They did enough," Gil said, chunking a stone into the river. "I never killed anybody before, Matt. Doesn't set too well on your stomach, does it?"

"No, it's bitter hard to swallow," Matt admitted. "My first

time was at Shiloh, first day. Oh, we'd been firin' volleys half the mornin', but there was so much smoke you couldn't really tell if you hit anything. Then we were rootin' Yanks out o' this hollow, and a couple of 'em made a rush at us. I shot the first one smack in the chest—killed him dead. Kyle dropped the other one. Wasn't time to think about it. We just shot. After, I went over and stared at that Yank. Shoot, he wasn't any older'n me. He hardly had a whisker on his chin. There was a tintype of a girl in his pocket.''

Matt paused long enough to cough away the emotion and wipe his eyes.

"So what'd you do with the picture?" Luke asked.

"Put it back," Matt explained. "Swapped out guns with the fellow as he had a rifle and took his cartridge belt. Then I followed the lieutenant.''

"He wasn't the last that day, was he?" Gil asked.

"May not've been the first. It rained that night, and I swear the ground seemed to be bleedin'. There were more dead men 'round than I want to think about.''

"Well, that war's over," Gil declared.

"Is it?" Luke asked. "The way that Yank cap'n talked, you'd never know it. How many folks've we seen chased off their farms? Folks're still dyin' o' that war.''

"Takes time to forget . . . and even more to forgive," Matt told the others. "But there's one thing I've learned. Time does pass. Wounds heal.''

"Not some," Linc said, shivering. Matt knew what Linc was thinking. Silvy would still be dead no matter how much time passed. So would Kate. Death carved deep scars sometimes.

Eli struck up one of Linc's mournful hymns, and the others joined in. The words might have provided comfort another time. Now they seemed somehow haunting.

"Miss you, Silvy," Linc whispered when the tune died away in the deep emptiness of the night.

"I miss you, too, Pa," Eli added.

"You, too, Ma and Pa," Luke said.

"Anna Louise," Gil whispered.

"Long day tomorrow," Matt declared after a few silent moments passed. "Best head back to the bunkhouse.''

"Matt, don't you . . ." Luke began.

Matt gripped his brother's shoulders and gazed across the river. "Miss you, Kate," Matt managed to mutter. Then he led the others back to the bunkhouse. He would keep a watchful eye out for One Eye that night, but somehow he knew sorrow would keep the Kiowas distant.

# CHAPTER
## ★ 5 ★

Matt labored long and hard with the new horses, working the wildness out and readying them for the saddle. Soon the corrals were full of good saddle horses. The ranch, however, was not overrun by buyers.

"Nobody has cash these days," Stump observed after driving the wagon to Jacksboro to pick up supplies. "Taxes just get higher, and there's no real work except on the cattle drives. I hear the mayor's wife's takin' in sewing in return for eggs and a little butter."

"Nobody's in need of horses?" Matt asked in disbelief.

"Oh, folks're in need of most everything," Stump declared. "Especially cash money to pay for things with."

Matt heard much the same thing as he and Gil led a string of ponies from settlement to settlement.

"Nice animals, all right," one barefooted farmer observed. "Be a big help to have a horse for plowin'. I can't pay you, but I'd see you got a share of the corn crop and a pig or two."

It was much the same everywhere. Soon Luke and Eli erected pens for hogs taken in trade, and a chicken coop was added afterward.

"Next thing you know we'll be takin' in wash," Stump grumbled.

"Not if they've seen the looks o' this outfit," Eli said, laughing. "Anyway, I kind o' like hogs. Bacon, anyway."

The hogs snorted angrily, and Luke scolded his friend for taking the feelings of the pigs so lightly.

"Next thing you know you'll have me singin' to the chickens," Eli complained.

"They'd really raise a stir then," Luke replied. "You don't have much of a singin' voice, Eli."

"Never knew a chicken to be real particular about such," Linc broke in. "Now don't you fellows have somethin' to keep yourselves busy? I got shoes to fit."

Linc carried the young wranglers along with him and set them to work building up a fire in the forge. Soon the ring of a hammer striking iron resounded across the land, silencing all other discussion.

Matt, meanwhile, did his best to barter or sell some of the excess stock, but he found no takers. Not long before he'd placed a forty-dollar price on even the more common range ponies. Now he was happily taking twenty-five, even less on occasion.

It was the same with other ranchers, too. Livestock plummeted. But Texans were nothing if not resourceful, and soon word spread of Saturday markets and livestock auctions.

"That's what we've needed right along," Stump grumbled. "Men biddin' for stock drives the price up, not down. Well, Matt, where's the first one to be?"

"Decatur this week," Matt explained. "Jacksboro the week after. I've been through both counties, and I wouldn't expect too much. The ranchers headin' north have their strings, and nobody else appears in a hurry to trade."

"We'll see," Stump said, scratching his head. "Might be best to take just the mustangs, though. Leave the colts and those good mares here. They'd make the start of a good herd."

"Providin' a man was inclined to turn serious horse breeder."

"Well, Matt?" Luke asked. "Isn't it time you did some settlin' down? Not so young anymore, you know."

"Young enough to throw you over one shoulder and carry you to the river for an early bath," Matt declared.

Luke kept a respectable distance from his brother for a while.

Matt merely laughed and set Gil to work selecting five horses to take to Decatur Saturday.

Matt wasn't counting a lot on the auction, so he wasn't terribly disappointed when only two buyers appeared. Neither was interested in horses. They came to buy chickens and hogs.

"Jacksboro may not be any better," Stump grumbled. "Maybe we ought to take a ride out west, toward Weatherford, or south to Ft. Worth. Might be some buyers there."

"We can always hope some outfit headed to Kansas will lose some horses," Matt added. "Long odds these, especially with Kiowas lurkin' about. Could be the best thing to do is split up, each man takin' a few horses to sell as he sees best."

"You can't send those boys off on their own, Matt," Stump argued.

"They could sign on with a trail herd," Matt suggested.

"And Linc?"

"Didn't figure you'd have any concern for him, Stump."

"He's a good enough man. Not many'd take in a real blacksmith, though, if you catch my meanin'. Likely he'd wind up workin' for the soldiers."

"Pay's regular enough."

"More to life than pay, Matt Ramsey. Man's got to have respect. Got to feel he's workin' his trade, too, not playin' out a short hand."

"True enough," Matt agreed.

The two men made a brief tour of the market before leaving. Matt bought a loaf of bread from a widow, some honey from a girl of perhaps ten, and a large ham from a pair of skeleton-thin boys whose tattered clothes and bare feet vexed him considerably.

"War orphans," a woman explained. "Live with their aunt, Miz Henry, but it's a hard life, I'd judge."

"Yes," Matt said, remembering how thin Luke and Bucky had been when Matt had returned from Vicksburg.

"Well, you goin' to stay here forever, or are we goin' to find a place to sit down and slice some o' that ham?" Stump asked. "I've got a hunger myself. How 'bout you?"

"I could eat," Matt admitted. But when they sat beneath a post oak and began slicing the ham, a small army of waifs descended upon them. The ragged youngsters said nothing, just stared hungrily at the food. Matt turned to Stump, who shrugged his shoulders. Moments later the children were chewing on ham or dipping corners of bread in honey.

"Not much of a trader, Matt," Stump declared. "You've got a good heart, though."

"You don't mean to stand there and tell me you wouldn't've done the same thing, do you?" Matt asked.

"Well, I never claimed to have a lick o' sense. You're supposed to be the smart one, Matt."

Matt was about to reply when a tall, raven-haired man clad in a long white coat, like trousers, and hand-tooled boots stepped over.

"I understand you've got some horses to sell," the man said.

"I do," Matt answered, "if the price's right."

"That's my very thought. Name's Max Clancy, and I run a few thousand head on the Bar C up north o' Millstown. Know it?"

"Can't say I do," Matt confessed. "Been there long?"

"Few months. Bought the place from the county. Terrible how folks lose good land for lack of cash to pay their taxes. Me, I plan to keep such places out of the hands of these money-hungry Yankee carpetbaggers."

"Must keep you busy," Stump observed.

"Does indeed," Clancy said. "Well, can I see your stock?"

"I've got five animals with me," Matt replied, "and a fine group back at the ranch if you'd care to ride out and have a look. Do you need breedin' stock or work ponies?"

"Remounts for my drovers," Clancy answered. "Plan to drive every longhorn I can into Kansas. I'll need mounts for my men."

"I've been gettin' thirty dollars a head," Matt said, leading the way to where the ponies were tethered.

"You haven't been gettin' that anywhere near Decatur," Clancy objected. "Best price goin's twenty-five, and you'll not see that again till next season. I'd pay ten perhaps."

"I'd eat a horse 'fore I'd give it away," Stump growled.

Matt then showed the horses. Clancy's eyes lit up straight away, and he examined the animals carefully.

"These are good animals, all right," Clancy admitted. "And I can see you know what you're about. I'll go to seventeen."

"Twenty, and that's as low as I'll sell a horse," Matt said, staring into Clancy's cold eyes. "You take that offer or give us leave to head home, Clancy."

"Can you have ten ready day after tomorrow?"

"We can have thirty," Matt answered. "You want us to bring 'em by?"

"I'll send my brother. What'd you call yourself, friend?"

"Matt Ramsey. You'll find us on the Trinity second bend west o' the Buffalo Springs crossin'."

"Well, Matt, it's a pleasure doin' business with you," Clancy said, extending his hand. "I'll have Bob out to your place with a bank draft for two hundred day after tomorrow."

"No bank draft," Stump protested. "Cash. Yankee greenbacks or silver."

"Very well," Clancy reluctantly agreed. "You'll have the horses ready?"

"Sure," Matt said, shaking the cattleman's hand. "Just you remember to bring the money."

"I don't generally let myself forget that part of a transaction," Clancy declared. "Hope to do business again with you real soon, Matt. You, too, friend."

Stump spit out a mouthful of tobacco juice and mumbled to himself.

"I don't care for that fellow," Stump told Matt as they mounted their horses and prepared to ride home.

"Why not?" Matt asked.

"He dresses too fancy by half, and he doesn't really look you straight in the eye. Mark me, Matt. You best see his money 'fore you sign over any stock."

"I will," Matt assured his companion. "I'm not so trustin' a fellow as you might think."

"None of us is these days."

Back at the ranch, the others received Matt's news with whoops and cheers.

"Some real cash at last!" Eli shouted.

Luke and Gil tossed hats in the air, and Linc began banging out a tune on his anvil. Soon even Stump cheered. Eli brought out the fiddle, and Stump began plucking and fiddling to high heaven. Matt uncorked a bottle, and a swig of corn soon had the whole outfit singing and shouting in celebration.

"Was there ever better news?" Luke asked.

"Many a time," Matt answered. "This Clancy's doin' us no great favor, boys. He's payin' low price, and he's gettin' top stock."

"He's payin' for ten horses, isn't he?" Luke asked. "Seems to me he's savin' us. We've got money to see us through winter if need be. As for prices, they're low everywhere."

"Not in Kansas," Eli said. "Maybe we ought to set off north. They say men make a fair life for themselves shootin' buffalo and such up on the Republican River."

"We're doin' all right here for now," Matt countered. "If you're hungry to see Kansas, Eli, Uncle Russ'll be through 'fore long. I'm sure he'll be eager to take you on."

"I didn't mean to say I wasn't happy here," Eli explained. "Just got an itch to move on some, I guess."

"I got one o' my own," Matt said, sending the bottle around a second time. "But just now I think this is a fair place to be. Company's not great, but then it's been a week since you had a bath."

"You, too," Luke said, nodding to the others. Matt was suddenly fallen upon, stripped, and dragged to the river. He managed to drag half the others in along with him, and soon the celebration moved to the water.

"Does my heart good to see those boys cheered so," Linc told Matt as they stood together on the bank watching Eli and Luke wrestle Gil to the shallows.

"Mine, too," Matt agreed. "Too bad it passes so quickly."

"What?"

"The good," Matt explained. "Seems like the brighter the smile, the quicker it fades. Kate was like that. I worry for Luke and Eli. Young Gil, too."

"They've done some growin' since I come here," Linc declared. "Got some more yet ahead. Still, I figure 'em for good men, the kind that stick to a thing till it's done. They're a lot like you, Matt."

"I'd wish 'em an easier trail than the one I've traveled," Matt said somberly. "But it's too late. They've each of 'em known hard times and death."

But as Matt listened to their taunts and watched their pranks, he cast those hard times from his mind. And he hoped the brightness would linger a bit.

# CHAPTER

## ★ 6 ★

The sun blazed through a thin haze Monday morning, showering the earth with a kind of golden glow. It promised to be an eventful day. Even as Matt readied the ten mustangs for Max Clancy, a teenage rider brought word from Buffalo Springs that a freighter was in the market for three horses. The boy handed over a letter that included four twenty-dollar greenbacks.

"Mr. Polk said you should send the horses along directly if the terms were fair," the boy explained.

"Fair enough," Matt said, turning to the others. "Stump, you want to take 'em? Give you a chance to buy some supplies."

"Give me that young Gil to keep me honest and half an hour to make a supply list," Stump answered.

No sooner did Stump and Gil leave than a Jacksboro rancher named Burton appeared with a second offer.

"We heard you showed some handsome horses over in Wise County Saturday," the rancher explained. "My neighbors and I need three or four ponies to make the drive to Kansas."

"We've got some good ones," Matt said, pointing to the corral.

40

In no time at all Burton selected four likely animals, then worked the price down a bit.

"Sure I can't talk you down under twenty-five?" the rancher asked.

"Not with half of Texas headin' up this way in a few weeks," Matt answered. "It's a fair price for those horses. They're sound as any you'll find."

Burton admitted as much, dug a roll of wrinkled banknotes from his pocket, and passed them over to Matt. A bill of sale was drawn up, and Matt dispatched Luke and Eli to help Burton manage the mustangs.

"Looks like we fell into some good fortune today," Linc observed as Matt stashed the money under the floorboards of the bunkhouse. "You got that Clancy fellow due in, too. Be fine to have some spendin' money for a change."

"Been a while, has it?"

"Long while. I hear a couple hundred dollars buys a nice farm these days. Might just make a fresh start, find myself a woman who ain't too particular about her man's looks and can put up with snorin'. I figure Silvy'd want me to."

"Never figured you for a farmer, Linc."

"Nor you for a mustanger, Matt Ramsey. But I guess the wind blows us to one thing or another, don't it?"

"Guess so," Matt admitted.

"I remember plantin' peach trees when I was, oh, fourteen maybe. Nice feelin' a man gets, plantin' things. Every spring when those little blossoms came to life, I'd feel good, even though I wasn't but a slave kept to hammer out shoes for a man what didn't even care if I was alive."

Matt thought of another peach orchard, the one at Shiloh where the lines of blue and gray dead intermixed in unearthly silence.

Linc noted the change in Matt's mood and stepped inside the bunkhouse for a moment. Matt was awaiting Linc's return when Bob Clancy rode up with four companions.

"You Ramsey?" the younger Clancy called out. Bob lacked both his elder brother's immaculate dress and quiet manner.

"I'm Matt Ramsey," Matt explained, offering a hand.

"Bob Clancy," the buyer's brother explained, spitting a mouthful of tobacco juice a few feet from Matt's toe. "Got some horses for me to look over?"

"Those ten over there," Matt replied, pointing out the mustangs.

"I figured to do the choosin' myself," Clancy objected. "Max didn't say anything about you pickin' out the animals."

"For twenty dollars a head, I pick the horses," Matt barked. "I told your brother as much. If you don't trust me, go home and fetch him along. I was told you'd bring the money and accept delivery of the horses, nothin' more."

"Figure me for a fool, Ramsey?" Clancy asked.

"I don't figure you at all," Matt answered, shaking his head. "It's a simple enough deal, and you got yourself a bargain price. Why make trouble?"

"Oh, I don't see any trouble, do you, boys?"

The others grinned and laughed among themselves. Matt grew alarmed, but Clancy climbed down from his horse then and stepped to the nearest mustang.

"These do look sound enough," Clancy admitted. "With times hard as they are, it's best to make sure you don't get cheated."

"Might do better to guard your words, too," Matt advised. "It could be that you might need to do business with me again one o' these days."

"Oh, don't take it personal, Ramsey. I don't know you. Pays to be cautious. If my words offended, forgive 'em. I had little schoolin' what with the war on and me considerably distracted with the fightin'."

"You signed the muster book, did you?"

"Fifteenth Arkansas Cavalry, me and Max both."

"I never heard o' that outfit."

"We were an independent regiment, attached to General Sterling Price. Mostly we rode up in Missouri against them Kansas raiders."

Matt soured. Many a thief and bandit profited himself by waving a Confederate banner and robbing anyone or anything he could find. Texas was full of Missouri families driven out by Yankee raiders or Ozark bushwhackers.

"You must've been with the regulars, I guess," Clancy said, sensing the disapproval in Matt's eyes. "Likely you were a captain or some such."

"Corporal, Second Texas," Matt said.

"Good outfit," one of the riders declared. "Close to wiped out at Corinth, then surrendered at Vicksburg."

"That's right," Matt said, studying the youthful face of the speaker.

"My uncle, Ben Chester, served in Company E," the rider went on. "I'm called Reb 'cause o' the war, though my Christian name's Ruben."

"I knew Ben," Matt said, grinning at the young man. "Was a good man in a fight, and even better when you were foragin' for food. He could make a chicken pop up from nowhere, I do believe."

"That's him, all right."

Reb Chester dismounted, and the three others followed suit. Clancy waved them to the corral. Matt motioned Clancy there as well, and for a time the men spoke of the war, of friends lost, and a people struggling to survive.

"Max's been doin' his best to loan money to folks so they can hold onto their land," Bob explained. "If they can't, he buys 'em out 'fore the county takes the land by force. Yeah, these are hard times, true enough. But these Yankees won't stay down here forever. Once the Kiowas and Comanches are run down, the cavalry can go squat."

"I guess your brother's doin' well with his cattle," Matt commented. "Must be to have money to lend."

"Oh, he's done fine enough," Bob declared. "But then . . ."

Bob Clancy froze when Linc stepped out of the bunkhouse.

"Matt, you still jawin' with those folks?" Linc asked.

"Got to take your time doin' business," Matt replied.

Clancy said nothing. Instead he waved his men toward their horses, then stared sourly at Matt.

"What's *he* doin' here?" Clancy asked.

"He works here," Matt answered. "That trouble you, does it?"

"Ought to trouble you a lot more," Clancy argued. "You mean to say he . . . he's part o' your outfit? Does he sleep and eat with you?"

"I admit it's a hardship," Matt said, forcing a grin onto his nervous face. "He snores somethin' awful. As for the eatin', Linc hasn't complained too much."

"You couldn't pay me a thousand dollars to have one of 'em in *my* bunkhouse," Clancy declared. "You crazy, Ramsey? You just fought a whole war to keep 'em in their place. Now you want 'em to take on white man's work while our own kids go hungry!''

"Wonder if there's any more of 'em 'round?" one of the riders asked. "Figure we ought to root 'em out, Bob?"

"I wouldn't," Matt warned, touching the cold handle of the Colt revolver strapped to his hip.

Linc retreated to the safety of the bunkhouse, and Matt hoped the big Sharps was in plain sight. Clancy stepped back, opening up the distance between them. The others knelt behind the corral. Matt glimpsed a pistol in one of their hands.

*A fine hole you've jumped down this time,* Matt told himself. *Five to one, and not so much as a pecan shell to hide behind!*

"I don't understand you, Ramsey," Clancy finally said. "He's not worth dyin' for. You touch that gun, you and he'll both be dead. Me, I kind o' like the notion."

"You'll die, too," Matt assured Bob Clancy. "Devil's likely clearin' out a space for you right now."

Clancy waited a moment. Then, shrugging his shoulders, he waved for his men to relax. Matt sighed with relief as well.

"If it's all the same with you, I'd like to get this business concluded and see you gone," Matt declared. "Well, Clancy? I've got the papers all drawn up. All that's needed is the money."

"I got that right here," Clancy said, counting out five twenty-dollar bills and slapping them in Matt's outstretched hand.

"Well?" Matt asked.

"You been paid," Clancy said, shouldering Matt aside as he motioned for his companions to grab the horses.

Matt turned and angrily grabbed Clancy by the arm.

"What's this about?" Matt cried. "The price I made your brother was twenty dollars a head. You owe me the other half . . . now! I don't offer credit."

"I don't need it," Clancy said with blazing eyes. "You're lucky to get that much. Horses that've been worked by darkies aren't worth any more."

"You must take me for a fool, Clancy!" Matt shouted. "You don't like the price, leave the horses."

"I don't think so," Clancy growled, continuing toward the horses. Matt reached out and wrestled Clancy to the ground.

"You really in a hurry to die?" Matt asked.

"Are you?" Clancy asked.

The four Clancy hands sported rifles, and Matt stared hard at them. He had a talent for calculating odds, and four rifles offered only the slimmest of chances. Even if Linc got one of them, and Matt managed to pull his pistol and get a second, there were two rifles left to deal with.

Matt fingered his Colt, but Reb Chester aimed a rifle and scowled.

"Mister, I'd sure hate to shoot a man soldiered with my own uncle, but I'd do it," the young man declared. "Toss that handgun away, easy if you please, and leave the boss to get his feet back."

Matt hesitated a moment, but he saw not a hint of indecision in Chester's cold gray eyes. Matt threw his gun away and let Bob Clancy escape. Clancy stumbled to his feet and glared at Matt with hateful eyes.

"You made yourself a mistake, Ramsey," Clancy declared. "I'll see you dead!"

Clancy reached for the discarded pistol, but the Sharps barrel protruding from the bunkhouse doorway drew his attention instead.

"That's right, mister!" Linc called. "I got your pretty white face lined up real fine. You best leave 'fore I forget the Lord's commandments and have me some fun."

"You fire, and he's dead," Clancy declared, pointing at Matt.

"Be a poor trade, a good man for the likes of you," Linc answered. "But then you wouldn't be around to think much on it, I suppose."

Clancy stepped back from Matt. The four rifles remained in place, though. The odds were as poor as before.

"We'll be leavin' now," Clancy said, drawing a paper out of his pocket and shoving it toward Matt. "Just sign the bill of sale, and we'll ride on. You see to it our paths don't cross again, though, Ramsey. I'll kill you sure."

"Oh, we'll see each other again, all right," Matt countered as he let the paper float away. Clancy retrieved it and passed it back to Matt, together with a pencil.

"Sign it," Clancy insisted.

"And the other hundred?" Matt asked.

"Oh, that's been settled already," Clancy insisted. "Now sign."

Matt glanced again at the rifles.

"You spit on your brother's honor, you know that?" Matt asked Clancy as he scrawled his name on the paper.

"I don't feel honor-bound by the likes of you and your darky outfit," Clancy said, stuffing the paper in his pocket and turning away.

"I have a long memory," Matt called as Clancy and his hands gathered the horses and set off for Millstown. "Clancy, you hear me? The wind has a way o' blowin' a bad smell back at a man in time."

Clancy only laughed as he led the way toward the river. Two hands guarded the retreat.

*There'll be another time, Clancy,* Matt silently promised. *That's apt to be the most expensive mistake you ever made!*

Matt waited in boiling silence for the others to return. Linc joined him on the top rail of the corral, but they shared no words. Matt's eyes stared furiously toward the tracks left in the muddy bank by Clancy's riders.

"Hundred dollars ain't so much," Linc finally mumbled.

"Enough to buy a farm, mold a future, you said," Matt answered. "Wouldn't matter if it was ten cents, though. A man either collects his debts or he doesn't."

"And you figure to settle with this Clancy fellow?"

"I will," Matt vowed.

When the others returned, they found Matt restlessly pacing alongside the corral. He already had his horse saddled. The Sharps was tied behind the saddle, and an extra pistol was stuffed in Matt's belt.

"What happened?" Eli asked.

Matt stomped off toward the river, leaving Linc to explain. Afterward, Matt's voice wasn't the only one to rise in anger.

"They can't just steal our horses!" Gil shouted.

"Didn't steal 'em, boy," Stump replied. "You signed their bill of sale, didn't you, Matt? Well, no sheriff's goin' to take our side against a big outfit like the Bar C."

"Isn't for any sheriff to settle," Matt grumbled. "It's for me to deal with. I'll ride down and have a talk with the Clancys."

"You figure Max'll hand over the rest of the money?" Luke asked.

"Be snow in August 'fore that'll happen," Linc declared. "Get yourself shot's all, Matt."

"It's not worth it," Luke added.

"Some things just got to be done," Matt argued. He fetched the roll of banknotes from the bunkhouse, added the new bills, and split it evenly among the six of them.

"Matt?" Luke asked, confused.

"It's still early in the season," Matt explained. "Uncle Russ'll need hands to take the trail to Kansas. Luke, Eli, Gil, he's sure to hire the three of you. Look after each other."

"And me?" Stump asked.

"Stump, half the ranches north o' Waco are lookin' for good, steady men. You won't have any trouble findin' work."

"Let me go with you," Stump argued. "Good company's hard to come by, and I'm old enough to know my own mind."

"We'll all go," Luke suggested.

"No, it's for me to settle," Matt insisted. "Luke, if you don't hear from me by August, you send this along to Amos," Matt added, handing over his bankroll.

"What about the rest of the horses?" Eli asked.

"Sell those you can," Matt suggested. "Each of you take a couple o' spares along. Kansas is a fair way, and you'll need good mounts. What you can't take, leave in the corrals. I plan to be back, you know."

"And if . . ." Luke began.

"Then you pick 'em up on your way through to Wichita," Matt said, shuddering slightly as he read the gloom in Luke's eyes.

"Matt, this is pure foolish," Luke said, grabbing his brother by both arms. "Chargin' into a fight's one thing, but you don't stand much of a chance takin' 'em on all alone."

"Oh, you'd be surprised how much one man movin' in the shadows can do."

"Matt, don't," Luke pleaded.

Matt gazed grimly at his younger brother, then led Luke to the river.

"It's a personal thing," Matt said, resting a hand on Luke's shoulder. "It was me those rifles were aimed at."

"It was *our* horses," Luke countered. "I'm not a kid anymore, Matt. None of us are."

"I've buried a lot o' my family since Vicksburg, Luke. Back in the war, I saw boys aplenty die who thought they were old enough. Guess they were. Don't need to be eighteen for a bullet to cut you down. You, Gil, Eli . . . you're all my brothers. It'd be nice for once to think o' you growin' tall.''

''I'm middlin' tall right now,'' Luke said, frowning.

''Yeah, you are, little brother,'' Matt admitted, managing a smile. ''Watch those longhorns now, hear?''

''Matt?'' Luke called as his brother started toward the saddled pinto waiting at the corral.

''I've got business to settle, little brother,'' Matt said, pausing a moment before continuing toward the corral. ''You look after yourself, Luke. Lots o' worry on the trail north.''

Luke nodded, and Matt climbed atop the horse. Then, waving sadly, Matt Ramsey set off into the shallows of the Trinity.

# CHAPTER
## ★ 7 ★

Matt rode southward. The sadness in his heart soon melted away, and a fiery rage replaced it. He spit a sour taste from his mouth and nudged his horse into a gallop. As he bounced along in the saddle, his mind filled with the taunting face of Bob Clancy.

*You don't know it, Clancy, but a world o' trouble's ridin' down on you,* Matt thought. And he knew, too, that he'd return with the promised hundred dollars, or someone would be dead.

Recollections of other fights—fruitless charges at Corinth and desperate battles against hooded marauders—flooded Matt's memory as he rode toward Millstown. For the first time in months, he was alone, and the silence of the empty countryside threatened to engulf him. And yet there was a freedom that came with independent action. There were no young wranglers looking to him for guidance, no frightened recruits waiting for Matt Ramsey to lead the way.

Matt followed the dusty road until he was a mile or so short of Millstown. He then made his way across the crumbling sandstone hills past town, keeping to the shadows of post oaks and scrub cedars. On the eastern side of town, a makeshift gate of crossed cedar logs marked the front gate of the Bar C. In truth, it was difficult to distinguish where the ranch began and the wild, seemingly endless plain ceased. Matt rode onto the ranch with growing caution. Up ahead a faint mist mixed with dust raised by restless longhorns. Matt nudged his horse into a shallow ravine and vanished from view.

For close to two hours, Matt remained out of sight, waiting for dusk to arrive. In the intervening hours, Matt scouted the ranch, taking care to locate the range crews. Most of the hands were scattered across the range, but the Clancy brothers, a trail cook and two cowboys were gathered beside a small fire at what was surely a roundup camp.

As darkness cast its veil upon the Texas plain, Matt made his way slowly, deliberately toward that camp. He rode like a phantom, eyes afire, the Sharps still tied behind his saddle. Long-barreled Colt pistols occupied each hand.

The first to block his progress was a smiling youngster whose ill-fitting clothes and oversized hat gave him an almost comical appearance. The boy held a Springfield rifle, though, and Matt found little amusing about his challenge.

"Who's there?" the youngster called, raising the rifle to his shoulder.

Matt slid off his horse, then crept through the brush until he could approach the boy from the rear. Then, with scarcely a sound, Matt leaped onto the back of the sentry and forced him to the ground. The cowboy attempted to shout an alarm, but Matt stuffed a kerchief in his mouth, then used the youngster's own rope to bind him.

"They'll find you in the mornin'," Matt assured the fearful cowhand. "You'll fare better'n some."

Matt led his horse along to within fifty yards of the camp. The two cowboys had set off to tend to some chore or another, and the cook was busy with his kettle. Matt tied his horse to a scrub cedar, then approached the fire.

"What's that?" Bob Clancy called in alarm.

"Armadillo ruttin' about most likely," his brother Max declared. "Expectin' Comanches or somethin', Bob?"

"Never can tell," Bob answered nervously.

"No, you can't," Matt added, stepping out of the shadows into the faint light of the campfire.

"What brings you to my camp?" Max asked, gazing at the drawn pistols.

"I come because I took you for a man o' honor, Clancy," Matt explained. "I come for what's due me."

"What'd that be?" Max asked.

"The hundred dollars your brother there cheated me out of," Matt said, glaring at the brothers.

"A fair sum," Max admitted, "but hardly worth gettin' killed for."

"So I'd say," Matt agreed, drawing the hammers of his pistols back with his thumbs so that the resulting clicks caught the Clancys' attention. Then Matt aimed a pistol at each brother's head.

"I paid you all you're entitled to," Bob argued. "I got the paper right here to show it's so."

Matt stepped closer, then slapped the bill of sale from Bob's hand. The paper flittered to the ground, and Matt kicked it into the fire.

"That won't get you very far, Ramsey," Bob warned. "I got witnesses, you know."

"Hang your witnesses," Matt countered. "I want the money that's owed me."

"Or what?" Max asked. "I got twenty men workin' for me. You fire one shot, and they'll be on you like a gob o' horseflies."

"You'll never know," Matt said, staring at the Clancys with blazing eyes. "You'll be dead, the both of you. As for your twenty hands, if they're all like the one I ran across earlier, they're more likely to shoot each other than bother me."

"There are some good boys out there, Ramsey," Max said, taking a step closer to the fire. "But there's little point to all this. Give him what he wants, won't you, Bob?"

Bob Clancy nodded, then opened his coat so as to draw something from a pocket. Then, quick as a cat, Bob dove for cover. A rifle barked from the shadows, and Matt felt something hot slap his left leg. Max scurried for safety, too, leaving the cook, fumbling with a pistol, to take Matt's fire.

"Boys, we got a visitor!" Max cried.

In minutes figures raced toward the camp, firing pistols wildly so that the nearby longhorns began to stir restlessly. Matt dragged himself along to the cover of a ridge. There he tore open the leg of his trousers and used the cloth to bind the wound.

"Fools, stop your shootin'," Max barked. "Let's get organized. He can't get very far on one leg."

Matt frowned. His horse pawed the ground twenty feet away.

With the cowboys crowding around their camp, Matt limped to the horse, untied the Sharps, and led the horse to a nearby ravine. It provided a fine hiding place for the pinto, and from the rim Matt could spy the roundup camp in the faint light of its cook fire.

"We'll see how you like this, Clancy," Matt muttered as he took aim and rammed back the rifle's heavy hammer. The sights rested on Bob's chest, but at the last minute another man moved in front and received the ball intended for the scoundrel.

"Lord, where'd that come from?" Max cried as the crew scattered. The booming blast from the Sharps startled the longhorns as well. The cattle were skittish before. Now they surged into motion, starting a stampede that soon sent several hundred cattle racing westward out of control.

"Bob, you settle accounts with our friend there," Max ordered. "I'll take the range crew and cut off the stock before they race all the way to Mexico."

In the ensuing confusion, Matt reloaded his rifle and set about locating Bob Clancy. The fire was no longer a help, for fearful cowboys had kicked dirt over its coals. The fight was little more than groping about in the night now. Clancy had the advantage of numbers, but Matt had experience and fury on his side. Matt crawled closer until he spotted a solitary figure gesturing wildly. The Sharps exploded, and the figure cried out in alarm.

"Give me some help!" Bob Clancy called. "He barely missed my head. Henry, Reb—get after him, boys!"

Clancy appeared to dig himself a hole. His companions opened up a brisk fire, and soon lead balls began tearing at the leaves of the nearby trees. Matt reloaded and fired again toward the younger Clancy.

"I saw the flash!" a cowboy called. "He's up past that ravine yonder."

"Go get him!" Bob shouted frantically.

Four of them did just that. Matt set aside the rifle and watched as the cowboys raced toward him. Matt waited until they were close, then rolled to his right and opened up with both pistols. The first two onrushing cowboys fell like rag dolls. The third stumbled, then managed to drag himself to safety. The fourth turned and fled.

Soon, though, others concentrated their fire on Matt. He had trouble even locating Bob Clancy. As the rifle fire splintered wood and shattered rock, Matt found himself retreating. Worse, he heard men circling around toward the ravine. He felt like a rabbit, trapped by enclosing hunters. There was no escaping. All that remained was the final, desperate fight—and the dying.

Well, Matt had faced death before. He wouldn't be easily rooted out of his hole. There was the one regret—that the Clancys weren't paying the price he'd set.

"He's just up ahead!" a voice called. "At the rim of the ravine, I think."

"Let's get him!" another shouted enthusiastically.

Matt never knew how many charged forward. He only saw the two straight ahead. He shot the first in the shoulder, then hit the other in the leg. Matt turned quickly to his left and saw two figures swing rifles his way. They were less than ten feet away, firing point blank. Matt gritted his teeth and waited for the blast that would kill him.

Instead a shotgun exploded behind the cowboys. Both were torn apart by the blast, and their rifles fell harmlessly to the ground. Matt watched in disbelief as the surviving cowhands dragged their fallen comrades to safety and cowered behind what rocks and trees offered cover.

A solitary shape crept toward Matt. While frantically reloading a shotgun, the somber eyes of Linc Stokes answered the question flooding Matt's mind.

"Knowin' your way o' goin' at a thing bull straight, I thought you might need some help," Linc explained as he took position beside Matt.

"You're a fool, Linc," Matt muttered.

"Seems to be a pair of us. A free man's entitled to be what he wants, you know. And I figure I still owe you for Buffalo Springs. Like as not, this business is on account o' me, too."

"No, this is Clancy's doin'," Matt said, bitterly gazing into the darkness.

"So, how's it to be done?"

"We either wait 'em out here or carry the fight to 'em."

"I never was much for waitin'," Linc said, breathing deeply.

"Nor was I," Matt confessed. He, too, took a deep breath, hoping somehow that would fight off the cold feeling gnawing at his gut. It didn't. Instead he led the way forward, over the rim of the ravine and on toward the camp.

This was no Vicksburg siege, no sweeping charge like at Corinth. It was cold, creeping death, and it left Matt uneasy. Still, he continued crawling closer. He could feel Linc's massive shoulders at his side, and that was somehow reassuring. Soon they passed the limp body of one of the charging cowboys. Another rested just ahead. So, they'd taken a toll, all right. But the real enemy still awaited.

Matt spotted Bob Clancy, but Clancy had eyes, too. He fired first, and his companions followed suit. In seconds the ground was torn apart by shot. Bullets tore his coat. Behind him they did deadlier work.

"Linc?" Matt called.

"Not much luck today," Linc answered, struggling to his feet so as to face his attackers. A rifle sent a ball into the big man's chest, though, and Linc Stokes fell dead. Matt felt something sting his shoulder. A searing pain then flashed through his forehead, and his vision blurred.

When he regained his senses, he found himself staring at Bob Clancy's gloating face.

"See, Max, we got 'em both!" Bob boasted. "That big darky and the reb fool, both."

"You lost too many men," Max complained. "Would've been better to pay the money. One o' these days you'll box yourself into a fix I can't get you out of."

"You can hire on more men, Max."

"Good ones? Half of Texas'll be headin' north soon, and you've left me shorthanded. The herd's scattered from here to tomorrow, and . . ."

Matt didn't hear the rest. He gripped the pistol resting in his right hand, rolled over and shouted, "Clancy!"

Bob turned, and Matt sent the smiling devil on his way to the nether region. Turning the pistol on Max, Matt tried to stand on his wounded leg. His shoulder felt warm with blood, and his forehead remained on fire.

"I got no more patience!" Matt screamed. "I want the money—now!"

"You shot my brother," Max growled.

"I'll shoot you, too, in half a second!"

Max shuddered, then drew the hundred dollars from his pocket and placed it in Matt's bloody, outstretched left hand.

"I need my horse," Matt added. "And one for Linc."

"He's dead," Max muttered.

"Get 'em!" Matt yelled.

A pair of cowboys scrambled to fetch the animals. Matt took care neither got behind him. He then had Linc's lifeless body tied across the Bar C horse while Matt climbed atop the pinto.

"As you said, Clancy," Matt said as he clutched the reins with the sweating fingers of his left hand, "a hundred dollars is a poor sum for a man's life."

"We have another debt to settle, Ramsey!" Max Clancy responded.

"Not this day," Matt said, glaring angrily at the surviving Clancy. "We've got graves to dig, you and me."

As he rode away, Matt kept the pistol aimed behind him. Leading the other horse along, he soon melted into the darkness. Broken and bleeding, he rode on.

"No, Linc, a hundred dollars isn't much to show for a man's life," Matt whispered. "Not for as good a man as you. But at least you're with your Silvy now. And me, well . . ."

Matt didn't complete the thought, for he was nowhere. The cold ate at his belly once more, but he continued onward. There was nothing else to do.

# CHAPTER

## ★ 8 ★

A great weariness overwhelmed Matt Ramsey a few miles north of Millstown, and he made his way up the side of a ridge and hid the horses in a grove of locusts. He left Linc Stokes's lifeless body atop the restless horse, for there seemed to be no strength left in Matt to do otherwise. He barely managed to unfurl a blanket before collapsing.

Matt drifted in and out of a troubled slumber as the sounds of horsemen searching the plain below roused him. His head continued to ache, and by morning his leg was swollen purple. The ball that had torn a slice from his shoulder had failed to lodge in the flesh. The bullet that grazed his forehead would have brought death another inch to the left.

Morning dawned bright and clear. It seemed too fine a day to dig a grave, and yet that was what Matt set out to do. He had no spade, so the best he could manage was a shallow trench cut out of the rough sandstone with a knife.

"You deserve better, Linc," Matt mumbled as he slipped the lifeless body of his friend into the grave. "But then who ever gets what he deserves in this life?"

Matt filled in the trench with loose dirt, then covered the grave with rocks to keep prowling wolves from disturbing it.

"You spoke of a debt," Matt said when the last rock was in place. "Well, Linc, I'd say it was paid in full."

Matt then etched Linc's name on the trunk of a cedar and left that as a marker. His leg was beginning to fester, and he could barely mount his horse. He sent the Bar C pony scampering off onto the plain, then turned his pinto back toward the Trinity. The horse sensed its rider's will, or perhaps smelled water. Whatever the reason, the animal galloped toward the river.

Matt only half remembered nudging the pinto along the river toward the bunkhouse. Afterward, a fever blurred his vision, and he scarcely recognized day from night. The horse reached the corral, though, and Matt fell out of the saddle and sprawled on his back near the bunkhouse.

"So, Clancy, you killed me after all," Matt mumbled as a pair of slight figures approached from the river. He felt hands reach down and lift him from the ground. A scent of lilac favored his nostrils, and he tried to blink away the haze before his eyes.

"Kate?" he muttered. "Kate, have you come for me?"

A soft hand touched his bloody shirt, and he warmed.

"Rest easy," a delicate voice advised. "You're in good hands."

"Kate?" he called again. "Ma?"

The voice spoke again, but Matt's feverish brain made no sense of the words. His eyes closed, and he lapsed into a deep and untroubled slumber.

Matt awoke to the sound of hammering. He blinked open his eyes and tried to rise, but his arms lacked the power, and he had no feeling at all in his legs. His head seemed bound in a vise, and as he moved a bit to one side, he realized linen bandages covered his forehead.

"What . . . how . . ." he managed to mutter before a dizziness hushed him.

"Ma, he's come to!" a shrill voice called, and rushing feet betrayed the arrival of his rescuers. Matt managed to force his eyelids apart enough to behold a slender-figured woman of forty or so leaning over the bed. His shoulder was bound in the remnants of a muslin shirt, and his body from the waist down was cloaked by a white bedsheet.

"Hello," the woman said as she touched her fingers to Matt's head. "You seem to have fallen upon misfortune."

"More like it fell on me," Matt grumbled. As his senses came back to him, he recognized the familiar surroundings of the bunkhouse. A strange assortment of blankets and linen covered the other beds, and a small army of children gathered at the foot of the bed.

"You'll mend," the woman pronounced. "The fever's finally broken. I drained the shoulder yesterday, and we'll try the same thing with your leg a little later."

"There's a bullet in there," Matt explained. "Maybe you can send . . . I mean, there's a doctor . . . Jacksboro . . ."

"Rest easy," she said, restraining his efforts to rise. "I cut the bullet out myself. Truth is, I probably did a better job of it than one of these frontier horse doctors would have."

Matt gazed into her china-blue eyes and managed a faint smile. He could feel his toes now. At least nobody'd cut off the leg.

"I don't remember much," Matt mumbled. "Who are you? How'd you come to be here?"

"We lost a wheel," she explained. "My boy Hugh located this place. Wasn't anyone about, but there were horses in the corral. We figured someone would come back, but . . . well, we couldn't very well abandon the wagon, and the children welcomed the roof. It rained quite hard the past two nights, you know."

"Rained?" Matt asked. "I don't . . ."

"You weren't in much of a state to," a speckle-faced boy in his early teens commented. "Slept half a week now, you have. Close to bled to death, I'd guess."

"Was Monday I got shot," Matt said, reliving the events in his mind. "I come back here . . . Tuesday."

"Mister, we'll take your word for that," the woman said, laughing. "We haven't known the month, much less the day, since leavin' Dallas. My Charles's gone ahead to locate us a farm. The children and I followed along, at least till we lost the wheel."

"We only stopped here 'cause it seemed nobody was around," the boy added. "Didn't mean to move in on you, but we thought maybe . . ."

"Doesn't matter," Matt interrupted. "Lucky for me you happened by. I'd a bled to death, sure. Or else they'd a found me."

"You're not a wanted man, are you?" the boy asked. "Your guns smelled o' heavy use."

"I'm Matt Ramsey," Matt explained. "I suppose there are those who'd like to lay hands on me, but none of 'em wear a marshal's badge. It's only fair, you know, they killed my partner. They wouldn't deal any too kindly with you folks, either."

"This *is* your place, isn't it?" the woman asked. "Hugh thought so because your horse wears the same brand as those in the corral. Still, we couldn't be sure."

"My partners and I had ourselves a mustangin' camp here," Matt explained. "Got cheated on a deal, and I went to set it right. Collected what was owed me, together with a bit o' lead."

"I knew he wasn't a bad man," a wide-eyed girl of perhaps thirteen said, sitting at the edge of the bed. "I could tell. He doesn't have the eyes of a killer."

*If only you knew,* Matt thought.

"Well, Mr. Ramsey, it appears the good Lord's seen fit to bring us together. I'm May Morley, and these are my children. Pardon their curiosity, and forgive their unwelcome attentions. They're new to the frontier, and I'm afraid they've been raised on tales of wild Indians and vicious outlaws."

"Well, you watch where you ride hereabouts," Matt advised. "There's some o' each ridin' the Trinity country."

"Indians?" the boy asked, raising his eyebrows.

"Kiowas," Matt explained. "They'd take your horses and your supplies, though they're less likely to bring the youngsters harm than some would say. Still, it's best to take precautions."

"And outlaws?"

"Thieves," Matt grumbled. "Too many of 'em set loose on the plains once the war was over. Not enough honest work, I guess. Most'll be watchin' the cattle trails now, hopin' to steal some beeves or pick off an army paymaster."

"Hugh, maybe it's best you boys stay closer to the house here," Mrs. Morley warned.

"Can't swim with Martha Ann and Liza lookin'," a younger boy Matt hadn't noticed before complained from the doorway.

"There's a fairly deep hole just th'other side o' the work corral," Matt said. "Sheltered by oaks. Ma'am, you give the eldest one o' my pistols just in case, though."

"That'd keep Liza's eyes to herself," the boy at the door said, laughing.

"Then if that's settled, you children have work to do," May Morley declared. "Mr. Ramsey needs his rest."

"You said maybe I could bring him some broth," the girl said, gazing eagerly at her mother.

"In a while, Liza," May replied. "Now, back to work, young ones." The children set about their varied tasks. Matt closed his eyes and let a peaceful sleep carry him away.

When he reawakened, the bunkhouse was bathed in the golden glow of candlelight. May Morley and her children gathered around the small oaken table at the far end of the single room. A stew bubbled on the stove, and its aroma swept the musty odors of old horsehide and perspiration from the place.

"Ma, look," a tall, yellow-haired girl said, pointing to Matt. "He's come around just in time for my stew."

Two small boys raced over and stared as Matt raised himself from the bed. His bandaged right shoulder was stiff, and his left leg ached considerably. He'd been hurt before, though, and he knew the pain was only part of the healing.

"Don't bother moving, Mr. Ramsey," May called. "I'll have Liza bring you something. She's been pleading with me all day to let her offer you some broth."

"I'd be obliged," Matt responded as he drew the sheet against his bare chest and dragged himself into a sitting position.

A younger girl arrived shortly with a bowl of stew, and Matt feebly tried to grip a spoon with his right hand. Pain flooded his face as he tried to work the torn muscles of his shoulder. He took the spoon in his left hand and managed better. In time he raised a spoonful of stew to his mouth and let the tasty bits of beef, potatoes, and carrots salve his hunger.

"Pure wonderful, ma'am," Matt called as he tried a second bite.

"I cooked it," the taller girl announced proudly.

"But I brought the bowl over," the younger one insisted.

Matt nodded to both of them, then continued eating. Each spoonful seemed to revive a powerful hunger, and the stew warmed him. When the bowl was empty, Liza rushed to refill it. Matt managed to empty that as well. Then he lay in the bed and allowed himself a moment of peace.

A bit later May Morley appeared and formally introduced the children. In addition to Martha Ann—tall and pretty as her mother, and Liza—thirteen and apple-blossom pretty, there were four boys. Hugh, the eldest, was freckle-faced and thin for four-teen. The three youngest, Bryant, Trent, and Joe Lee, were as alike as brothers could be, stairstepped in height as suited their ages. There was much of their mother in the children's faces, and they had all inherited May's flaxen hair.

Matt greeted each in turn, giving a weary left hand to Hugh and Bryant. The children then readied themselves for sleep, and Matt marveled at the way May Morley drifted from bed to bed, listening to prayers or offering reassurance. It brought back to Matt the years of his own childhood spent in a barracks of a back room with four brothers.

He closed his eyes and listened to the subtle sounds of the youngsters stirring in their beds. He felt like an intruder in their peaceful world. Oh, they had their worries, true enough, but there were comforts in having family.

Matt grew more envious in the days that followed. It wasn't long before he was able to get around with the aid of a crutch.

"Know anything 'bout wheels, Mr. Ramsey?" Hugh asked the first time Matt hobbled outside.

"Somethin'," Matt said, making his way to where Hugh and his brothers had managed to prop the back of their wagon onto two water barrels. Both rear wheels showed signs of cracked spokes, and the iron rims were sprung.

"Are they bad?" Hugh asked.

"Bad enough," Matt confessed. "I could work the spokes some, but I got no talent with iron. Bet you can get a couple of wheels made for you in Jacksboro, though."

"Sure, we can," Hugh muttered. "Man at the livery there said he'd fix 'em for us for ten dollars."

"And you thought they'd last till you met up with your pa?"

"Wasn't that," Hugh said, staring at his feet. "I ain't seen ten dollars in my whole life."

"I have," Matt said, reaching into his pocket and taking out the bankroll. He peeled off a ten dollar greenback and passed it to Hugh.

"I can't take money," the boy protested.

"You can't get that rim reshaped without a forge," Matt said, frowning as he thought of Linc. "And a man who knows how to work iron. Take a spare horse and keep to the main road. Watch out for trouble, and see to it you get proper wheels for your money."

"Ma'll have a fit if she finds out I took money off you," Hugh argued. "She's none too happy we're stayin' in your house."

"You don't figure savin' my life's earned you anythin', do you? I'd a bled to death sure if you folks hadn't come by. Now get on a horse and head for town. Leave the arguin' to me, will you?"

The boy failed to budge, and Matt frowned.

"Pride's a fine thing," Matt said, staring at his stiff leg. "Close to got me killed, you know. I owe you and your ma, Hugh, and this is my way to pay you back. I'd ride down there myself, only I figure I'd fall off my horse a mile down the trail. Now, why don't you saddle a horse and get on along?"

Hugh looked up, then glanced at the wheels. He nodded, and set off toward the corral.

"I got no saddle horse, you know," he called.

"I got a corral half full of 'em," Matt said, motioning toward the eight horses nervously pacing the corral. "Any one of 'em's apt to be glad o' the exercise."

Hugh picked out a charcoal mare and located a saddle. As he tied the wheels on the back of a white gelding, Matt turned and hobbled to the bunkhouse.

May Morley was less than delighted that Matt had sent her son into Jacksboro, but Matt merely shrugged his shoulders.

"It needed doin', ma'am," he explained. "A week ago I had a man with me who could've fixed your wheels, but he's gone now. I'd be obliged if you'd let me do this by way o' thankin' you for all the good food and attention."

"The food's mostly yours," she answered. "But I suppose it's done now, and there's no use worrying over it."

Hugh reappeared late that afternoon, and Matt helped the boys fit the mended wheels on the back axle. Then he joined them at the river for a twilight scrub.

He sat at the table that night and shared dinner. He said nothing, just listened to the excited children talking of resuming their journey.

Afterward, Matt limped out to the river and watched the stars dancing across the ebony darkness overhead.

"Kate, we might've had all that," he whispered, closing his eyes and seeing her herding a handful of kids to the creek. The scene evaporated as he recalled standing beside the grave as her walnut casket was lowered into the earth. It wasn't just Kate

Silcox they'd buried. Matt's hopes and their dream of a better life was also nestled in the cold earth of Fannin County.

Early that next morning, the Morleys crowded into their wagon. Matt offered them a pair of horses to ease the journey, but May would have none of it. The children waved a sad farewell, and Matt acknowledged their good-bye with a silent nod. Then the wagon vanished in a swirl of traildust.

He missed the noise straight away. The children's laughter, the thoughtful attentions of Liza and Martha Ann, the admiring gazes of the boys . . . their absence left Matt hollow. And as other families rumbled by in oxcarts or rickety wagons, Matt recognized his own despair etched in their defeated faces.

He rode into Jacksboro himself and dispatched all but twenty dollars of his remaining funds to his brother Amos.

"From your brother Matt," he scratched on the accompanying note.

He then climbed atop his horse and headed back toward the Trinity. Nothing awaited him there, and that thought left him cold and hollow once more. Loneliness gnawed at him, threatened to swallow him whole. And he saw no brightness waiting on the far horizon.

# CHAPTER

# ★ 9 ★

Mid-May brought the first rush of trail herds making their way north toward Red River Station and the distant railheads of southern Kansas. Great swirling clouds of dust that threatened to choke the sun rose from beneath the flood of longhorns. From time to time a crew watered their herd near Matt's place on the Trinity. Now and then a cattleman would purchase a spare horse. By June Matt had only three animals, including the pinto, left in his corral.

Russ Ramsey's Circle R outfit came along shortly thereafter. The Circle R herd watered fifteen miles downstream, and Matt might never have known of their passing had not Luke ridden up one afternoon.

"Didn't know if I'd find you alive or not," Luke said, swallowing deeply as he climbed off his horse and walked to Matt's side. "Pure crazy ridin' off alone like that, Matt."

"Seems so now," Matt confessed. "Gil and Eli ride with you?"

"Yeah," Luke said, grinning. "The three of us kind o' got used to each other, I suppose. Shoot, even old Stump's along.

Everybody but you and Linc. I guess Linc figured he'd brought enough trouble our way.''

"Linc's dead," Matt said, staring southward.

"What?"

"Followed me to the Clancy place. Saved my life, Luke. Fool! Wish I could've returned the favor. I saw him buried, though. It's all there was left to do."

"Well, leastwise he's not lonesome anymore."

"Guess not," Matt agreed. "Heaven's full o' his people. And ours."

"Yeah," Luke muttered, staring at his toes. For a few moments the brothers stood beside each other in awkward silence. Then Luke managed to speak. "We're short two men of havin' a full crew," he said. "Matt, you'd make up for both of 'em. Uncle Russ'd take you on and thank you for comin'.''

"It's a long trail leads to Kansas," Matt observed.

"True enough, but the company's fair, and Uncle Russ's got himself a trail cook that bakes close to's good as Ma did."

"I got need o' solitude just now," Matt said. "If you make the trip and don't drink yourselves to death in some Wichita saloon, stop by on the way south."

"You'll still be here?"

"Or close by. You know me. One place's as good as another."

"Matt?" Luke said, gripping Matt's hands and silently urging him to ride along.

"You got a long ride north, little brother. Time you was off."

"I told you I'm not so little these days," Luke argued. "You weren't goin' to call me that anymore."

"Well, it's a problem we old-timers have," Matt said, grinning. "You wait and see if you don't have the same problem when Bucky gets his growth."

"He won't ever get it," Luke said, swallowing a sadness as he mounted his horse. "Fool boy's goin' to reach into the oven one too many times and burn his hands down to stumps. Or else some farmer'll catch him snatchin' melons and unload a shotgun into his backside."

"You survived, didn't you? So did I, for that matter, and Buck's not half so bad as either of us."

"Not so good at gettin' by, either," Luke said, laughing. "We'll be by, Matt, the three of us. Who knows? Maybe the

market for horses'll improve, and we can go after mustangs
again.''

"Could be," Matt said without conviction. "Watch yourself,
Luke. Stay clear o' those border raiders.''

"Always do," Luke declared as he rode away.


As the herds continued to surge northward, Matt spent more
and more of his time stalking the Trinity hills, hunting and fishing and fighting off an engulfing gloom. Sometimes he'd share
a campfire with some trail crew. Another night he'd bring a
string of catfish to some family camped on the river, swapping
a fish supper for a bit of company.

Mothers and fathers sometimes whispered about "the strange
fellow with the game leg," but Matt didn't pay them much attention. He warmed when the children greeted his tales with
smiles and laughter. And if he seemed to appear and then vanish
somewhat mysteriously, he knew that made the stories all the
better.

Not all the camps Matt visited welcomed him, though. Twice
farmers aimed shotguns in his direction, and once a young cowboy put a hole through Matt's hat. Toward the middle of the
month, Matt discovered two hands cut down by hatchets, stripped
bare, and left to the buzzards. Matt gazed on the bloody business
with a heavy heart. Neither cowboy was much older than Luke.
Matt covered the bodies and sent word to their companions.

"Hard luck," the trail boss grumbled. "Like as not Kiowas
did it. Probably cut beeves out of the herd, too. I'm short men
and time both, mister. If you'll bury 'em, there's five dollars in
it for you.''

"Keep your money," Matt said bitterly. "I just thought maybe
a boy's life was worth a moment's pause and a few words from
a friend.''

He knew, though, that most cowboys were like himself, men
drifting through life, getting by as they could. No one much
celebrated their coming or mourned their going.

One Eye's Kiowas were particularly busy that summer. Aside
from worrying trail herds, they set half of Millstown afire, shut
down the stage line north of Jacksboro, and twice hit army supply trains. Matt only heard of those exploits from passing riders,
of course. He saw firsthand the handiwork of the Kiowas later
on.

It was a clearer morning than usual. The sun rose high and bright, casting a glitter on the river and baking the sandy clay soil hard with its unrelenting heat. Matt remembered such days growing up, how he and his brothers would work the corn and cotton fields under that fiery sun. He only lived for the chance to soak his tormented body in the creek at dusk.

Another year Matt might have passed the entire afternoon in the river, but swimming reminded him of the afternoons with the Morley boys, brought back the fine times he'd shared back home and later with his mustanging partners. In no time he'd be remembering Kate, so instead Matt took his rifle and set off into the hills in hopes of locating fresh meat for the kettle.

He spotted a pair of squirrels a mile and a half from the bunkhouse, but instead of taking aim, Matt paused to watch their antics. All in all, squirrels were pretty useless creatures, and they multiplied nearly as fast as rabbits. Matt wasn't very sympathetic toward them, but his spirits were strangely raised by those particular animals.

It was well he didn't shoot. The brush just ahead stirred, and a band of young Kiowas rode by on horseback. One Eye wasn't among them, but their ponies were painted for war, and their boastful mumblings hinted that something was afoot.

Matt soon discovered what it was. A hundred yards up the trail, two wagons lay trapped in a sandy bog. Men lashed oxen in hopes of pulling the sunken wheels from the mire, but the wagons failed to budge. Children pleaded with the animals, and women fretted.

"Lord, help 'em," Matt mumbled as he made his way past the Indians in hopes of warning of the enclosing danger. He was too late, though. A terrible howl split the air, and six Kiowas charged the wagons, waving hatchets and chasing the frightened children into the bog. Matt gazed in horror as the Indians struck down one of the men as he raced for his rifle. The other turned and fled into the brush, but a young Kiowa ran him down.

The women dragged their youngsters through the mud, screaming and praying at the same time. One had a small pistol in her hand, and she managed to discourage her pursuers by firing the gun whenever anyone got close. A boy of fifteen or so suddenly turned and rushed toward the wagons. Perhaps he wished to rescue a father or fetch a rifle. Or maybe the boy simply lost his head. Whatever, it availed him little. One Eye appeared as the young man neared the wagon, and the Kiowa leader dispatched an arrow that felled the boy instantly.

Matt shifted his eyes from the wagon. He knew no one could help that boy. The women and little ones remained in peril, though, so he headed in their direction.

All battles, from the smallest skirmish to the largest campaign, are mostly confusion, and Matt took advantage of that fact to make his way to the edge of the bog.

"Here!" he called, waving the fleeing settlers to his side. "Hurry!"

Matt's voice was calm, confident, and the others followed his orders instinctively. The younger children were befuddled, but they followed their mothers. The women saw in Matt's Sharps rifle their delivery from the rampaging Kiowas. They asked no questions, just ushered their children into a rocky ravine while Matt prepared to dissuade the Indians from following.

Most of the Kiowas busied themselves rifling through the wagons, taking what supplies might prove useful and scattering all other possessions to the four winds. It was unbridled chaos, and Matt knew it plagued the hearts of the settlers to watch the treasures accumulated in a lifetime strewn about like worthless scraps of nothing. Still, he was glad of the distraction, because when three Kiowas started toward the ravine, he was ready for them.

He set the Sharps aside and fired first with his pistol. The shot was aimed well over the heads of the Indians, and it accomplished its purpose. The Kiowas drew up short and gazed back at One Eye.

"What're you waitin' for?" one of the women called. "Kill the devils!"

"They murdered my John," the second added. "And Lord knows what they did to Stephen."

"I can't kill 'em all," Matt muttered. "Want I should drop a couple and leave the rest to scalp you? My way, I'll see you safe through this."

A small child started whimpering, and Matt instantly regretted his hard words. But they were necessary, and as true as any he'd spoken. Still, another man might have omitted the harshness.

One Eye spoke to his young companions harshly. He was clearly displeased with them and said as much. Then, waving his bow over his head, he led them toward the ravine. Matt lifted the Sharps to his shoulder and waited for a rider to fill the sights. A youthful face, painted death black, rode forward, and Matt fired. The big-bore rifle did its work well, and the young Kiowa's neck snapped backward as the bullet struck home. Matt handed the rifle to a youngster and drew his pistols.

"Well?" Matt asked as the boy stared at the smoking rifle. "Don't you know how to load a rifle?"

"I do," one of the women said, taking the rifle from the terrified boy. Matt passed over a cartridge pouch, and the woman reloaded the rifle as Matt prepared to engage the Indians with his pistols. He never had the chance. One Eye gazed at the fallen warrior, then stared wild-eyed as Matt rose, ready to kill again.

"Enough!" Matt shouted. "You understand? No more!"

One Eye hesitated, and Matt took aim. The Indians then turned and rode off, fetching their dead companion as they went.

"Here," the woman said, shoving Matt's rifle at him. "Get the chief. He's out there all alone now."

Matt saw One Eye slowly riding back and forth between the wagons, babbling away in a mixture of Spanish phrases and what must have been the Kiowa tongue. Matt understood nothing of it. Then One Eye vanished, and Matt turned to offer what comfort he could provide.

"Leave us," one of the women growled as Matt helped a young girl to her feet. "We got dead to tend."

"I can help," Matt offered.

"You helped us about enough," the other woman added. "Why didn't you help our men? They lie up there dead, likely scalped, and you fire warnin' shots!"

Matt left them to their sorrow. He was an outsider, after all, and if they didn't want his protection, so be it! Let One Eye come back and butcher the lot of them!

Matt never shot the squirrels or anything else for the table. He was content to make a meal of jerked beef and cold biscuits. It was a far cry from one of Martha Ann Morley's stews, but then he really had no appetite that night.

He found no rest when he took to his bed that night. He was again haunted by the terrified faces of those children. He heard their mothers' hard words, and they tore at him like the sharp talons of a red-tailed hawk.

The sounds of the horses whinnying in the corral first drew

his attention. They were generally quiet on a moonlit night, but just now they stormed about the corral uneasily. Next Matt heard splashes down at the river. And there were subtle rustlings of leaves, twigs snapping, and the like.

Matt pulled on his trousers and buckled on his gunbelt. Next he took the Sharps from its place beside the stove. In seconds he was standing in the door of the bunkhouse, rifle ready, and eyes peering through the darkness for signs of trouble.

Matt knew without thinking that he had visitors. He also knew they were Indians. Another man might have slept right through their visit, awakening, if at all, to discover his corral bare. Matt sensed their presence, though, and he stepped out into the open and headed toward the corral. A pair of shadows attempted to slide the top rail back and allow the horses to escape. Matt raised the rifle and fired. Both figures fled in panic.

While he reloaded his rifle, Matt kept watch for the others. One Eye would never send a pair of boys out alone to raid horses. Not from Matt Ramsey anyway.

*Perhaps,* Matt thought, *they don't know this is my place.* That wasn't likely. One Eye seemed aware of everything.

That very moment five horsemen charged through the river, howling and firing rifles no doubt acquired from the settlers at the bog. Matt darted behind Linc's forge, then opened up with both pistols. One rider was flung from his horse, and a second howled in pain. One Eye then rode out and waved the others back.

For a moment, the bare-chested leader remained in the shallows, staring at Matt with cold hatred. Moonlight illuminated the scarred bronze face.

"One Eye," Matt called, stepping out to face the Kiowa.

The two of them gazed across the open ground, their cold, hard eyes examining each other for some sign of weakness. In the end, a kind of mutual respect seemed to flow from one to the other and back again.

"We meet again," the one-eyed warrior finally called in broken English. He added other, foreign, words then finished with a Spanish phrase that chilled Matt's blood. "Muerte." Death.

The Kiowa wasn't issuing a threat, Matt realized. He was naming his enemy.

"You're right," Matt mumbled as the Indian turned and rode

away. "Muerte—death. That's me, all right. Death is the one trade I know best, and it's the path I've traveled most often."

No one was there to hear those words, not even a scarred old Kiowa. Instead they drifted on the wind and were swept off into the emptiness that lay beyond the Trinity.

*Yes, I'm death,* Matt told himself as he stumbled wearily to the bunkhouse. It wasn't what he intended, what he'd hoped for.

"See what's happened to me, Kate?" he called to the stars. "See what I've become?"

There was no soft touch to ease his suffering, though. No quiet voice offered solace or comfort. There was only the icy solitude of the bunkhouse . . . and the cold reality of what had come to be.

# CHAPTER

## ★ 10 ★

Summer's close brought other visitors to the Trinity. Gil and Eli rode in first, followed a minute later by Luke and a smiling, sandy-haired twelve-year-old.

"The three of us thought you might be hard up for help," Luke explained, "so I rounded up this stray out in Fannin County. Said he figured you needed a bit o' prankin' to raise your spirits. Me, I think he just wanted to muster out o' the farmin' business."

Matt gazed up at the boy. He'd grown tanned as old leather from the July sun, and his legs seemed to stretch halfway out of the stirrups. His hair was wind blown and a little shaggy, but the grin was all too familiar.

"You goin' to sit up there all afternoon, Buck," Matt asked, "or are you goin' to jump down here and greet your brother proper?"

The youngster instantly gave out a war whoop and leaped onto Matt's shoulders. Matt paused a moment to let his brother's weight settle. The left leg had been slow to heal, and it buckled some under the pounds Bucky had added that past year. Soon enough, though, Matt was carrying the boy down to the river.

"Oh, no, Matt," Bucky pleaded as his elder brother swung to the right, then pitched the boy into the Trinity. A roar of laughter greeted Bucky's abrupt baptism, and soon the whole batch of them were peeling off dusty clothes and splashing into the stream.

"You been carved up some since I saw you," Bucky said, touching the faint scar on Matt's forehead and the darker one across his shoulder. "Luke said there'd been some trouble."

"You know me," Matt mumbled. "Trouble has a way o' findin' me."

"More like you findin' it," Luke complained. "Anyway, I figure a bunch o' rich drovers like us ought to make good company for a renegade mustanger, eh, Matt? Price o' horses goes up weekly, I hear."

"In Kansas, maybe," Matt grumbled. "Not hereabouts. Nobody's got much cash for range ponies, and now the trail herds are 'bout finished headin' north, there's scant money or work, either one."

"Just as well," Bucky remarked. "I'm not partial fond o' work. Swimmin' and fishin' are more to my likin'."

The others hooted at the grinning youngster, and Matt couldn't help but laugh. They weren't any of them prone to bendin' their backs to work when they could sidestep it.

Those next few days a veil of gloom seemed to lift from the little ranch on the Trinity. Whether splashing away the heat of mid-afternoon or dipping lines in the river in search of catfish, Bucky and Luke seemed to breathe new life into their brother. Matt recognized the fact, smiled his gratitude, and walked with a quicker step and a lighter heart. Where before he'd ridden among the new ranches and farms with his horses expecting hostility and suspicion, he now greeted folks with an eager smile and bargained as a veteran horse trader should. As a result, he soon emptied the corral of the last few animals.

"Looks like we're low on stock, Matt," Luke observed. " 'Fore long, we ought to have ourselves a look out on the plains. Like as not there are mustangs runnin' around wonderin' what's become of us. Shoot, they got nothin' to do but get chased by ropers now the Indians've gone north."

"Who told you that?" Matt asked.

"Just figured the cavalry'd finished 'em by now."

"Not One Eye," Matt told the others. "He was by here in

June, whoopin' up a storm and makin' a try for the stock. That old Sharps convinced him to try elsewhere, though.''

''How'd it do that?'' Bucky wanted to know.

The others gathered around, and Matt set about telling the story of the bogged-down settlers, the Kiowas, and Matt's stubborn defense. He didn't mention Muerte. That other self seemed miles away just then, and Matt had no wish to call him back.

''We didn't have so easy a time of it ourselves,'' Eli said as Matt concluded his tale. ''Seems the Nations these days're full o' bandits. We were scarce across the Red River when the first pack hit us. Snarled like wolves, those skunks. Was a close thing holdin' onto the herd, but Russ wouldn't hear o' backin' out o' a fight.''

''After all, he's a Ramsey,'' Luke said, taking up the tale. ''Was twenty of 'em, I'd say, all carryin' those new repeaters and hot for seein' us bleed. They come on us at dusk, ridin' hard and doin' their best to turn the herd and scatter us in the bargain. Could've used that Sharps o' yours, Matt, 'stead o' pistols and nerve.''

''They shot ole Stump that day,'' Gil lamented. ''Cory Hardin as well. Might've bagged the whole crew 'cept the herd stayed with us. Then those blessed longhorns did turn—right on top o' the rustlers.''

''Three thousand horns come down on 'em,'' Luke said, swallowing hard. ''Wasn't enough left o' some o' those boys to bury. Wasn't any stoppin' the cattle once they busted loose.''

''Never saw a thing like that before,'' Eli said, soberly shaking his head. ''Was like a big hand reached out o' the sky and turned those steers. I've not been much on prayer since Pa got hung, but I swear I've taken it up again. Was a judgment, that stampede.''

''More like heat lightin',''  Luke insisted. ''Still, does make for a better tale told that way. Whatever, I didn't mind it much. Saved our hides for certain.''

Gil and Eli nodded their agreement. Bucky frowned heavily and leaned his shoulder against Matt. Instinctively, Matt placed a reassuring hand on his brother's back and tapped the boy lightly.

They shared other stories that night and swapped a few yarns before finally taking to their beds. Early the next morning, Luke again suggested it was time to scout the plain, and the five of them packed up supplies, gobbled breakfast, and saddled their horses. An hour past dawn, Matt was leading the way through the distant hills in search of mustangs.

It wasn't horses they found, though. Fifteen miles northwest of the river, Matt detected dark brown shapes dotting the plain ahead. At first he dismissed them as maverick longhorns, but as the distance closed between men and beasts, Matt noted the coloring was wrong. Moreover, the shapes seemed hunched awkwardly. A dank odor of dung and unwashed flesh swept across them, and Matt motioned a halt.

"Matt?" Bucky whispered, hardly restraining his excitement.

"Buffalo," Matt explained, gravely counting the beasts. "Twenty or so. Rare these days to find 'em so far south, what with hunters ridin' 'em down from the Dakotas."

"I never tasted buffalo meat," Eli said, gazing over at Matt. "Shoot, I only seen three or four of 'em in my whole life, and they were lyin' skinned and rottin' up in Kansas."

"Not many of 'em left nowadays," Matt told his companions. "Lots o' longhorns about, you know."

"I'm sick o' beeves," Gill muttered. "Been eatin' their dust all summer. I'll bet you could bring one down with that Sharps, Matt. Lend her to me, and I'll drop one myself."

"I always wanted a buffalo-hide coat," Bucky said, grinning. "Saw one once. Keeps the winter chill off, you know."

Matt stared at the grazing beasts. It was poor sport, closing in on the monsters and blasting away from long range. He'd heard tales of Comanches darting in and loosing arrows from five feet away. A thundering bull might gore a horse and trample its rider.

"I got my Springfield," Gil said, pulling the rifle from its scabbard. "Ought to do the trick."

"Should," Matt admitted. "But the Sharps was born to the task."

"We'll each take a turn," Luke said as Matt passed the gun along.

"We pack the meat home, too," Matt insisted. "No wastin' it like up in Kansas."

"We've need of winter coats," Eli said, hoping the excuse would bring Matt around to the notion. "And if we don't shoot, somebody else's sure to do it. Can't hide long, these hairy critters."

"Take two," Matt suggested. "More'n that, and the meat'll spoil."

"We could sell meat in Jacksboro," Eli suggested. "Lots o' folks would pay to taste real buffalo."

Matt shook his head, but the others seemed bent on felling five, enough for each of them to have a coat.

"So how do we go about it?" Luke asked, studying the herd. "Can't all of us shoot at once."

"No," Matt agreed. "Wind's in your favor, though. Thing to mind is that they don't turn and come back at you. Find some high ground, then spot the leaders. They'll circle some, givin' you time to shoot again."

"There's a hill just ahead," Eli said, pointing to a slope crowned by an outcropping of limestone. It provided a perfect stand, and Matt led his companions there.

After tying the horses securely in a grove of scrub oaks, Matt's band of would-be hunters started for the outcropping. The buffalo continued to graze below, ignorant of the encroaching hands of fate.

"Leave the cows be," Matt said, pointing especially to three brownish-colored beasts trailed by calves. "Take that big one on the right to begin with. He seems to be listenin' for trouble."

Indeed, a large bull moved anxiously along the fringe of the herd, lifting his shaggy head and shaking it as if that would help detect danger. The danger was too near, Matt knew, and when Eli took the Sharps and aimed, the bull was doomed. The rifle then exploded, and a fifty-caliber ball split the air, raced across the plain, and stopped the bull's massive heart.

Almost without thinking, Matt took the rifle, reloaded, and passed it to Luke. At the same instant, Gil fired his Springfield at a bull rumbling toward his fallen brother. Luke, too, fired, and a third animal dropped.

*They've learned the trade well,* Matt thought as he reloaded his rifle once more. Bucky cradled the Springfield, steadied it by resting the barrel on a rock, and fired. The recoil knocked the twelve-year-old off his feet, but the aim was true enough to fell another buffalo. Matt took the final shot himself as the herd finally set itself in motion. The lumbering creatures turned a slow circle as a new leader fought to emerge. Matt ignored the two bulls fighting their way through the others and aimed at a smaller buffalo stumbling along near the rear. He aimed and fired in a single motion, and the last buffalo dropped on his forelegs, then rolled on one side, dead.

"Shoot, Matt, I heard o' this," Eli said excitedly. "See 'em circlin'. A good hunter'd take the whole bunch this same mornin'."

"Can't wear but one coat, Eli," Matt grumbled. "And we can't tote more meat back without pack mules. It's enough. No, it's more'n enough."

Luke and Bucky nodded grimly as their brother drew out a skinning knife. The difficult task still lay ahead, and when the herd moved off at last, the younger Ramseys followed Matt to the slain buffalo.

It wasn't easy. In fact, peeling the tough hides from the buffalo was hard work, more like skinning a mountain than stripping the hide of a longhorn steer or a whitetail deer. It proved especially unpleasant work in the midday heat, and the smell soon overpowered them. Matt tied a bandana and placed it over his mouth and nose in the same way he'd often done to cut down the dust when trailing horses or cattle. It did little to sweeten the oppressive smell.

It wasn't long before the buzzards began to circle. Soon they would begin picking at the kills, and Matt hurried to cut away the hides and butcher the meat. Eli and Luke cut green ashes to make poles for making pony drags while Gil set the hides out to dry. The August sun sped that labor along considerably. Matt was glad of it, for the skinning grew more troublesome with each animal.

"I hear some outfits take twenty, thirty a day," Luke marveled as he worked to pack the meat. "One fellow said he dropped a hundred and five in one stand. Wiped 'em out, biggest bull to littlest calf."

"Calves, too?" Matt asked in disbelief.

"Seems small coats are popular, too. Boys wear 'em."

Matt scowled. He noticed frowns spreading among the others as well. It wasn't sport, after all, just cold, heartless murder. The army encouraged it, so he'd heard, knowing the plains tribes would starve without the buffalo hunt. Already the bands of Comanches that not long ago cut their lodge poles in East Texas had moved out onto the Llano or north onto the high plain west of the Nations in the Colorado Territory. The Cheyenne and Arapaho were already there, forced south by the invading Sioux.

*It's an old story,* Matt thought. *The Yanks did it at Vicksburg, after all. Box 'em up, then starve 'em into surrenderin'. It had worked in '63. Probably it would again.*

They were the rest of the day packing the meat and drying the hides. That night they returned to the ranch heavily laden with meat and began smoking the better pieces for use come winter. On the morrow, Luke and Eli would take the rest into Jacksboro to sell to rooming houses and eateries.

Once the meat was packed away or sold off, all that remained of the buffalo were five hides. Matt nailed them to the western wall and began cutting away what scraps of meat still clung to the parched flesh.

"Doesn't seem like there's much left of 'em," Bucky said as he helped Gil soak strips of oak bark. The resulting brown liquid did a fair job of tanning buckskin and cowhide. Matt hoped it would likewise preserve the buffalo hides so that coats could later be cut and stitched from them.

"Indians used every inch o' the buffalo," Matt finally told his brother. "Made bowstrings out o' the sinew, sewin' needles and such o' the bone, powder flasks o' the horns, and so on. I hear the tail makes a fair whip, and a knife can be fashioned from a rib."

"I almost wish we'd let 'em be," Bucky said, settling in at Matt's side. "Does seem poor justice, killin' off the last of 'em."

"Forgettin' your coat?"

"No," Bucky said, grinning. "I near froze last winter, you know. Be good to have the wind off my ribs. Still, I don't think I'd have been too sad to've missed my shot."

"I know," Matt said, nodding. "Life's full o' hard choices, Buck. A man's heart can't always call the tune. He's got a brain to use, too, and it reasons things out, sorts out the good and the bad, and sets him on his course."

"Leaves you sad sometimes, though."

"Does at that," Matt confessed. "But a man can't expect too much. If he's got a warm, dry bed at night, a full belly, a sound horse, and fair company, he's luckier than most."

"I got no complaints, Matt."

"Not even when you work the cornfields?"

"Well, I never took to that kind o' work anymore'n you did. I've come to be a mustanger and a cowboy now, though. No more choppin' weeds or huskin' corn for Buck Ramsey. Shoot,

I've got hairs growin' on my chin now. Another year, I'm apt to be tall as Luke.''

Matt examined the boy with a critical eye. A year? More like five or six by Matt's reckoning. What was it about Texas that hurried boys into their pa's boots?

Matt finished working the hides and motioned for Bucky to splash the tanning juice on. When the hides were all treated satisfactorily, Matt led his brother to the river to wash for supper.

That night Matt awoke to a fearsome howling. *Wolves*, he told himself. But when it continued, he slipped quietly past his sleeping companions, took the Sharps in his hands, and stepped outside.

A strange haze smothered the moon, and an eerie stillness possessed the night. The usual breeze off the river had been stilled.

Matt gazed again at the moon. The haze took on an unreal, elongated shape, its four wispy fingers taking on the appearance of flying feet. The great silver half-circle of the moon illuminated the whole thing, giving it a ghostly glow. And when the white disk rose above, the spectre seemed to grow a massive hump.

''Buffalo ghost,'' Bucky whispered, stepping to Matt's side. ''It looks like a buffalo ghost.''

''Yes,'' Matt agreed. ''Buffalo's about done for.''

The howling continued, and Matt thought he glimpsed shadows down by the river. The buffalo ghost charged across the heavens. And the cries? Matt wondered if they weren't the death chants of the Kiowas lamenting the passing of their way of life.

''What is it, Matt?'' Bucky whispered. ''Wolves?''

''Sure, wolves,'' Matt muttered. ''Likely pickin' at the bones of our dead buffalo.''

''That's awful far away, isn't it?''

Matt gripped the boy's broadening shoulders and shuddered. Sure it was far away, and the apparition in the sky was only a bit of cloud passing before the moon. That was all.

''Matt?'' Bucky asked, leaning back against his brother's chest.

''It's best forgotten,'' Matt advised. ''Just wolves.''

The boy was unconvinced. Matt wasn't surprised. He himself wasn't half persuaded.

# CHAPTER
## ★ 11 ★

While the buffalo hides dried on the side of the bunkhouse, Matt and his crew devoted their energies to running down range ponies. They scoured the countryside north of the Trinity for sign of mustangs, but mostly they returned discouraged and empty-handed.

"It's all the new folks," Gil observed. "Every stitch of the river seems to be swarmin' with women and kids. For now they're content to run longhorns or keep pigs and chickens, but by and by they'll plow up the grass and plant corn."

"Isn't just that," Luke said, eyeing Matt nervously. "I hear the soldiers've taken to shootin' mustangs, figurin' the Indians won't have remounts that way."

"Neither will they," Matt said, studying his brother's face. "You're serious, aren't you, Luke?"

"We rode past twenty or so of 'em rottin' in a ravine on our way north," Eli explained. "It's not so easy to run down a range pony, but shootin' one's no big worry with a big-bore rifle like your Sharps, Matt. Won't be horses runnin' wild here much longer if this keeps up."

"No way to stop it," Gil pointed out.

"First the buffalo and now the mustang," Matt said, staring at the setting sun. Kiowa ghosts indeed! They had a right to howl. It seemed the bluecoats aimed to paint over the character of the frontier, shape it so it was more to their own liking.

"Isn't just the Yankees, either," Gil added. "It's roads and trails that cut up the range. Towns that choke the streams with their leavin's. People are comin' west, whole armies of 'em. There's nothin' left back east for 'em but high taxes and heavy-handed judges. What freedom's to be found is beyond the Crossed Timbers."

"Then we're searchin' the wrong hills for horses," Matt pointed out. "We ought to pack up and head for the Llano."

"Sure, get scalped by Comanches," Eli cried. "I seen all the Indians I got a taste for on the Chisholm Trail."

"Well, what do we do, friends?" Matt asked, pulling his horse up short. "Stay 'round here lookin' for a few strays or ride west?"

"No corrals out that way," Luke pointed out. "Plenty o' trouble."

"Wasn't all that long ago we chased up thirty or so real regular," Matt reminded them. "Got to be a few dozen hereabouts. Let's find 'em, work 'em into saddle mounts, and make some money while we can. Sure as blazes isn't much ranch work to be had."

"Lead the way, Matt," Luke suggested.

They rode across half the hills in northern Texas that next week, but they only spotted three pitiful herds. The largest had seven horses, and Matt's mustangers only roped three of those. Another pair of spotted mares turned up on the way homeward, and a splendid, raven-black stallion was run down just shy of the river.

"Six horses," Bucky grumbled as he stared at the anxious horses prancing around the work corral. "Luke spins tales o' catchin' fifty, and all we rope is six!"

"You didn't even rope one," Eli said, pulling the youngster from his saddle. "Who knows, Luke? Maybe Buck here can talk 'em into takin' to the saddle. He's mighty good with the words, this boy."

Bucky lowered his head and charged into Eli with a force that sent the both of them rolling in the dust. Bucky lashed out with feet and fists with a fury that stunned Eli. As for Eli, the older boy didn't quite know what to do. He had the size and strength, but Bucky's energy overcame both. It was like grabbing hold of a miniature grizzly. The claws were as sharp as the real thing, and the rascal couldn't be outrun.

"Looks like you've got your hands full," Matt observed, laughing.

"Somebody pull him off," Eli pleaded. "I'll wind up layin' a good one on him."

"If you can find somethin' to hit under all that dust he's stir-rin' up," Gil said, slapping his knees as Bucky grabbed Eli's legs and twisted them until the mighty had fallen. Bucky, feeling triumphant, sat atop his victim and pronounced himself the vic-tor.

"Not just yet, you little toad," Eli said, rolling out from un-der Bucky's grasp, grabbing the twelve-year-old by a handful of hair and dragging him to the river. Seconds later a surprised Bucky was floundering in midstream.

"Now, mind you behave, Buck," Eli scolded. "I'd hate to start teachin' you manners this late in the season."

The others laughed, and Bucky's mouth opened wide. A sput-tered complaint issued forth, followed by a laugh of his own.

"Guess I showed him," Bucky remarked, shaking the water from his clothes as he walked out of the river.

Early September was devoted to working the range ponies into saddle mounts. For the most part, the horses proved little chal-lenge. The mares in particular seemed disposed of a gentle na-ture, and even Bucky was able to sit on them the very first week. Not so the big black.

"He's used to havin' his way," Luke observed as Matt battled with the powerful animal. The stallion stubbornly resisted the bit, and Matt began to wonder if the horse would ever yield to a rider. Matt had a stubborn streak of his own, though, and he hung with the animal, whispering to it when its hind feet took to flying and singing when the darkness began to fall.

"Can't devote a year to him, Matt," Luke finally declared. "We'd best head out again, run down another dozen or so before the county fills up with settlers."

"It's too late already," Matt grumbled. "We got neighbors on either side of us now, and any day now I expect some farmer to show up and claim the bunkhouse as his own. Time's about gone, I fear.''

"You figure we should pull up stakes, give up on her, Matt?'' Eli asked. "What'll we do?''

"It's a problem,'' Matt confessed. "You've each got some cash, I'll wager. Enough to keep you through the winter if need be.''

"Keep us?'' Gil asked. "I never passed a winter holed up in some roomin' house. I'd turn daft in a month. I got to have somethin' to keep myself busy.''

"Not many ranches hirin' on winter hands,'' Luke pointed out. "Me and Bucky'd be welcome with my brother Amos, I suppose.''

"He'd be glad of extra hands at harvest,'' Matt pointed out. "More'n likely he'd take the four of you.''

"What'll you try, Matt?'' Luke asked.

"I got the black to work a while yet,'' Matt answered. "Be another week or so at least gettin' him settled down. I'd judge some ranch's fool enough to take me on for the season, especially if I don't dicker much where wages are concerned.''

"We still got to sell the horses,'' Eli declared. "Maybe Gil and I ought to make the rounds in case there's work to be had. I'd settle for room and board plus a bit o' change. Come spring, there'll be lots hirin', with roundups and trail herds startin' up and all.''

"What about you, Luke?'' Gil asked. "You got money set by?''

"Winter's a lonesome season,'' Luke said, frowning. "It's a way off, I know, but Amos really could use me at harvest. It's been a time since I saw the old place, and Bucky ought to have a bit o' Rose Margaret's attention put to his readin' and writin'. Ma'd have a fit if she knew he was close to's illiterate as Matt!''

"As me?'' Matt complained. "I can read what I have a mind to. Bills o' sale, for instance. Never found time for books.''

"Or much else save wild horses and clear horizons,'' Luke grumbled. "Well, we'll head on back once we get the horses sold.''

"Do I have to go?'' Bucky asked.

"Gets too cold out here to throw you in the creek come winter,'' Matt explained. "What'd we do with you when you got crosswise, Buck, murder you? Wouldn't hurt to pass a bit o' time in a feather bed, would it? Rose Margaret's cookin' sure beats my stews.''

"She's a good cook, I'll grant you," Bucky agreed, "but she's powerful bossy. There's all o' those little ones underfoot, too.''

"You were one yourself not so long ago," Matt reminded him. "Now it's settled. Send a wire tomorrow when you take the horses in. Me, I'll stay and work the black.''

The other five horses, together with Matt's pinto, were sold off easily enough. Gil did most of the dickering, and he had no heart for it. Luke insisted on thirty-five and the rest for twenty-two.

"You send the wire, Luke?" Matt asked when the four riders reappeared at the bunkhouse.

"I sent it," Luke said sorrowfully. "We'll head out soon's you help get those buffalo hides cut and shaped into coats.''

"Rose Margaret'd be better at it than me," Matt said.

"She can do the sewin', or get us started," Luke countered. "Need you to do the shapin', Matt. You got a way o' puttin' a fine look on a hide.''

Matt nodded reluctantly and marked his brothers' dimensions on the hides. Then he cut the rough hide into assorted pieces, the body first and the sleeves thereafter. With the hides ready for sewing, Matt bade farewell to Luke and Bucky, promising to send word when he got settled.

"You watch yourself, Matt," Luke urged as he gripped his brother's wrists. Bucky said nothing, just wrapped a weary arm around his brother, coughed away a tear, and climbed atop his horse.

Eli and Gil stayed a fortnight longer. Each day they rode from ranch to ranch in search of work. Then, when they both began to despair, a tall, dark-haired ex-teamster named John Moss happened by with an offer.

"I hear you boys know stock," Moss told the three of them. "I need a man to watch my horses, and I've got another spot mindin' the cows. Can't pay a lot, understand, and I got eight kids that're like as not to drive you to drink once a day and twice on Sunday. Still, it's honest enough work, and you'll find I'm a fair man. I'll tell you what I think, and I won't hold it against you doin' the same.''

"There are three of us," Gil pointed out.

"Can't afford to feed you all," Moss explained. "Maybe another outfit'll take the other."

"I've still got this ornery horse to gentle," Matt said, smiling at his young companions. He felt suddenly old, gazing at their bright, clear eyes. There weren't but five years between him and Gil, but two of those had been spent fighting Yankees. They seemed to make a world of difference.

"You sure, Matt?" Eli asked. "I hate to think o' leavin' you like back in June."

"I managed then," Matt reminded them. "I will this time, too."

They turned toward Moss, who nodded. It took but a few moments more to collect belongings in a blanket roll, to tie the same behind their saddles, and finally ride westward toward the JM Ranch.

"My wife cooks up a storm Sunday 'round midday," Moss called to Matt as they reached the river. "You're welcome anytime."

"Thanks," Matt answered. "Might take you up on the offer."

"Do!" Eli called. "You'd be a welcome sight, Matt Ramsey."

Gil nodded his agreement, and the thought of Matt visiting somehow lifted the young riders' spirits. Once they were gone, Matt felt the keen edge of loneliness once more.

The midnight stallion stirred restlessly, and Matt climbed onto the top rail of the corral and gazed down at the frothing horse.

"You feel it, don't you, boy?" Matt asked. "Nothin' eats at a man like the lonelies. You miss the mares, don't you? I miss everything . . . the midsummer sun, the buffalo, the wild country you crossed usin' memory instead of by followin' some fool trail cut by wagon ruts.

"I miss the days when I could run as fast as you do and never got winded. I miss the creek back home. And I do purely miss Kate."

He listened a moment as the wind seemed to sigh an answer. A cloud moved across the sun, allowing its rays to burst golden bright from the western sky.

"So, you can't fight the bit forever, old friend," Matt said, jumping into the corral and walking to the stallion's side. Matt stroked the big horse's nose, then drew it close. The horse had never allowed more than a brush of contact, but now it seemed to welcome Matt's touch.

"Sure, you feel the lonelies, too, don't you?" Matt whispered. "What do you say I give you the bit, and you show me how a real horse carries an old fool like me? Eh?"

The animal whinnied an answer, and Matt gave the reluctant horse the bit, then pulled the bridle over his snout and ears. For a few minutes he allowed the horse to grow accustomed to the feel. Then Matt climbed atop the sleek stallion's ebony back, rubbing its neck and pressing his legs against the trim creature's ribs.

"Well, show me, Black!" Matt barked.

The stallion responded immediately, throwing back its feet, arching its back, and performing as wild a series of antics as any Matt had seen. He clung to the reins, grabbed a handful of mane, struggled to outlast the stallion.

"There now, have you finished?" Matt asked when the horse ceased its manic contortions. The two seemed as one, and Matt dropped his cheek against the neck of the powerful animal.

"You haven't lost anythin', boy," Matt assured the stallion. "You and me were born under the same moon, cut from like cloth. We're brothers now, the two of us. And you'll never feel spur nor whip from me."

The stallion dipped its head as if somehow it understood the words. Matt believed it so, for he stroked the stallion's flanks and whispered an old melody his mother had once sung:

> Now 'tis come the dawnin'
> Of a Hieland day,
> Now wee lads are yawnin'
> Soon to be on their way.

He sang of a place he'd never known, recounted manners and words stranger than the Kiowa taunts One Eye hurled across the Trinity. It wasn't the words that warmed him. It was the face he recalled that had shared those self-same words.

"Hold your head proud, Matt Ramsey," she'd told him the day he'd set off with Kyle and the rest of the recruits. "Neither turn your back on your friends or show your heels to the enemy. Stand as old Lachlan stood at Culloden—a boy, too, he was. You'll nay face half the trials that one did, I'll wager."

She hadn't known. Neither had Matt. It didn't matter. He'd weathered every storm and survived all challenges. Now he slid off the horse, gave it a gentle pat, and set off for the bunkhouse. It took him even less time to pack up his belongings than the others. Then, wrapping everything in the buffalo hide, he headed for the corral.

"You don't mind a bit more weight, do you, boy?" Matt asked.

He smoothed a saddle blanket out across the horse's back, then added a saddle. He left the cinch firm but not so tight as to trouble the ribs. Finally he tied his belongings in place and set off to fetch the Sharps. The big rifle was the final adornment.

"Farewell, not much of a ranch," Matt called as he slid the rails away, mounted the big black, and headed away from what had been as much a home as any following the war. He turned the stallion toward the river, then splashed across. Jacksboro was a bit farther on. He'd be there by supper.

# CHAPTER

## ★ 12 ★

Sitting atop the big black, Matt felt oddly revived. The horse had a raw energy, a power that urged Matt onward. He left the road and raced across country, feeling the wind sting his face and sweep the hair back from his tanned forehead. A new day had seemingly dawned, and suddenly Matt ceased to worry about the future, or about anything else for that matter.

He reached Jacksboro toward dusk. The ride had brought out a hunger, and he wasted no time in locating a small eatery on the far side of the town square. The building was of simple plank construction, and a simply lettered sign pinned to the open door was the sole hint that dinner was offered within. The aroma of fresh-baked bread drew Matt inside, and he followed a girl of perhaps fourteen to a long table and sat down on the bench.

"It's four bits," the girl said. "In advance."

"Don't figure I'm good for it, huh?" Matt asked, smiling as he drew out the requested money and set it on the table.

"We get a lot of no-accounts through here, mister," the girl explained. "Can't stay in business feedin' anybody with a hungry mouth."

"Guess not," Matt admitted.

The others at the table were mostly unmarried merchants or temporary visitors to the county seat. Matt recognized one of the army horse buyers at the far corner. His tailored coat and laced cuffs set him off from the others as much as did Matt's dusty boots and unkempt hair.

The cook and owner of the eatery was a round-faced woman with the pleasant name of Devona Pickworth. She served up a platter of baked chicken, assorted vegetables, and all the biscuits and honey a man could hope to force down his gullet. Afterward, there was apple pie spiced with enough cinnamon to delight even the most particular diner.

"Fine meal, ma'am," Matt said after swallowing the last of his pie.

Mrs. Pickworth smiled, nodded, and said, "Stay awhile, mister . . ."

"Ramsey, ma'am," Matt introduced himself. "Matt Ramsey."

"Mr. Ramsey, many of my gentlemen stay a bit after meals and share a cup of coffee. You're more than welcome."

Matt saw no like encouragement in the eyes of the other gents. He grinned, expressed his regrets, and slowly made his way to the door. Once outside, he untied the stallion from a hitching post and conducted the animal down the street to a livery. He found the twin doors to the stable barred, but candles illuminated a small room attached to one side, and Matt stepped to its door and knocked lightly.

"What you want?" a gruff voice called from the other side of the door. "I'm havin' my dinner."

"Got a horse to board," Matt explained.

"Leave him someplace and come back later. I got no time to fool with you now."

"I'll tie him 'round the side," Matt said. "He's fresh broke, though, and apt to be skittish where strangers are concerned. Might be best to leave him be till I get back."

"Expect me to feed him sugar an' honey, did you? Tuck him in and tell him a story? Leave me be and get along with you!"

Matt couldn't help grinning. Times might be hard, but here was a man who hadn't lost his head where business was concerned. First came dinner. Then his customers could expect attention.

"There's another place down the road toward the fort," a boy said, popping out from behind a nearby barrel. "He's a big 'un, ain't he?"

"Big enough," Matt admitted as the youngster touched the stallion's shoulder. The horse stirred anxiously, and the boy pulled away.

"Bites, I'll bet," he said nervously.

"Wouldn't be surprised if he doesn't eat tow-headed boys whole," Matt replied.

"Oh, me an' horses get on fair enough," the boy said, easing his fingers back toward the horse. The big black turned his head, and the youngster hopped back.

"Know where work's to be found?" Matt asked.

"Work?" the boy asked, taking off a weather-beaten brown hat and scratching his dirty hair. "If I knew, I'd not be sleepin' behind a barrel and beggin' such food as old man Fitzpatrick don't eat."

"Not a lot o' jobs for pee-wees, eh?" Matt asked.

"I'm nigh on twelve," the boy barked. "And I hold my own with anybody this side o' the Rockies!"

"Well, Mr. This-side-o'-the-Rockies, you can earn yourself half a dollar by findin' a bucket o' water for this horse here. And if your other labors don't take too much o' your time, you could watch my things."

"Glad to, Mr. Ramsey."

"I know you?" Matt asked, searching the boy's face for some familiar feature.

"I was out to the Jenkins place when you sold off those spotted geldin's last spring. I'm Culver Herrick, though most folks know me as Cully."

Matt took the boy's dirty hand in his own.

"Don't you have family, son?" Matt asked.

"Got an uncle somewhere 'round town," the boy said, his eyes dimming as he glanced up the street. "Pa fell someplace in Virginia, and Ma, well, she took sick thereafter."

Matt felt a chill work its way through him. Except for being half a foot shorter, that boy could have been Bucky. Matt fought to find a word of encouragement, or perhaps comfort, but he wasn't well acquainted with such sentiments. Instead he nodded to the boy, then set off toward the town's main street.

The army had started building Ft. Richardson along a wooded stretch of Lost Creek the previous fall, and Matt marveled at the way the post had changed the town. Jacksboro was growing up right and left, mainly along the old military road to abandoned Ft. Belknap and the better market roads south to Ft. Worth and north to Buffalo Springs. On the eastern fringe of Lost Creek, directly opposite the fort, a whole separate community known as Sudsville had come into being. At first the place was mainly a camp for the laundresses that seemed to haunt every frontier fort. Of late gamblers, whiskey merchants, and other enterprises devoted to entertaining soldiers and freeing them from their scant pay had set up tents and rough clapboard shanties.

Matt avoided Sudsville. Instead, he made his way from one business to another, inquiring after work. Many closed at dusk, and those with their doors still open looked upon Matt's dusty clothes and rough hands with suspicion or contempt. One woman chased him out the door with a broom, crying, "We've no need of your kind of riff-raff hereabouts!"

Matt finally drifted back toward the livery. There he finally met the cantankerous O. T. Fitzpatrick.

"You the fellow wouldn't let me eat in peace?" the stableman asked. "Ought to charge you double for the trouble."

"Didn't mean to be trouble," Matt said, glancing around for some sign of Cully Herrick. The big black drank from a water bucket, but Matt's belongings and saddle had vanished.

"I got a corral where you can leave your horse," the old man grumbled. "Dollar a day for board. Three days in advance."

"I may not stay that long," Matt explained. "I'm lookin' for work."

"You'll be here a month lookin' for anybody to hire you on," Fitzpatrick said. "You give me a dollar honest money, and pay right along as you stay."

"You see a boy 'round here?" Matt asked. "He was to watch my gear."

"You'd be a bigger fool than I thought to trust the mites in this town with anything worth money, mister."

"Name's Matt . . . Ramsey," Matt explained. "Didn't seem a bad sort to me."

"Likely wouldn't be if his ma hadn't got herself scalped by Comanches or if some fever hadn't kilt his sister or the war taken his daddy or some such. Town's full o' sad tales lately. I'd judge you to have one o' your own. Man's got no time to listen to such these days. Leave me a dollar, and I'll see your horse gets some oats. Elsewise be gone and leave me to my work.''

Matt handed over a silver dollar, then set off down the street in search of his belongings. He got no more than a hundred feet when he saw his saddle propped against the wall of a saloon. Cully sat atop a nearby barrel chatting with a peg-legged slouch of a man clad in ragged woolen trousers and a threadbare tunic that before being patched beyond recognition had belonged to a Confederate officer. A kepi tilted to one side of the ex-soldier's head.

Matt started toward the former rebel, but before he could get closer than fifteen feet, a trio of drunken soldiers accosted the veteran.

''And here we thought we'd chased all the rebs to hell!'' a tall corporal cried. ''Here's one we missed.''

''Well, we got a part of him,'' a dark-haired private said, sliding his boot over so that the graycoat's good leg bent back, causing him to fall hard against the wooden decking in front of the saloon.

''Leave him be!'' Cully screamed, pouncing like a wildcat on the back of the dark-haired Yankee. The corporal reached out, plucked Cully from his companion, and dragged the boy to a dirty watering trough.

''This 'un needs a good scrub!'' the corporal declared, slinging Cully into the trough.

Matt had seen enough. A voice inside him whispered that no real harm had been done, that a bit of water would not, in truth, hurt Cully Herrick one bit. But even as prudence suggested otherwise, Matt charged the drunken soldiers.

''Hey, friend, watch where you put your hands,'' the corporal said when Matt pushed the soldiers away and helped a sputtering Cully from the trough.

''Maybe he wants a bit of a wash himself,'' the third soldier suggested. Younger, with straw-colored hair, he reached for Matt, missed, and found himself booted out into the street.

Matt then bent over the fallen soldier. One sniff told all. The ex-Confederate had also visited the saloon. Matt helped the man rise, then turned as the corporal swung a heavy fist toward Matt's jaw.

Matt managed to deflect the blow, but a second landed squarely in his ribs. Fury and frustration merged, and Matt grabbed the corporal by the throat, shook him angrily, and heaved him out into the street beside his blond comrade.

"Look out!" Cully cried as the dark-haired private swung a board across Matt's back. The plank struck hard and sudden, sending Matt to the ground. The private lifted a leg and prepared to stomp a heavy boot into Matt's face, but Matt rolled sideways, grabbed the soldier's belt, and drove a shoulder into the blue-coat's midsection.

"All right now," Matt said, kicking the gasping private into his companions. "You really want someone to beat on, come try me. I got two legs, and I'm full grown. Three of you ought just about to make a fair fight of it!"

"Hold there!" the burly saloon-keeper urged, stepping out the doors. The soldiers either didn't hear or didn't care to. They charged Matt in tandem, flailing away with their drunken arms like rag puppets in a miniature theater. Matt met fist with fist, and weeks of battling the black stallion had put iron in his hands. He felt the sting of blows, tasted the blood from a battered lip, but his own fists felled one bluecoat after the other until the three of them floundered in the dusty street.

Matt reached down and plucked his discarded hat from the street, shook the dust from his clothes, and started toward his saddle.

"No!" Cully cried.

Matt instinctively ducked as the corporal raised his pistol and fired. The first bullet nicked the wall of the saloon, sending onlookers diving to the floor. The second whizzed past Matt's ear and slammed into the arm of the saloon-keeper. The third exploded in the chest of the peg-legged veteran, dropping him into the onrushing arms of Cully Herrick.

Perhaps the bloody sight of his handiwork or maybe the hateful eyes of the townfolk prevented a fourth shot. Or it may have been there were but three cartridges in the pistol. Whatever the reason, the shooting ceased. As Matt blinked away shock and pain, one of the girls from the saloon tended her wounded boss while two others knelt over the dying ex-rebel.

"Ab?" one of them whispered. "Cap'n Ab?"

The captain only rolled his eyes toward Cully, managed to grin, then died.

"Murderers!" the boy screamed. "Kill 'em!"

"It's all *his* fault," the corporal argued, pointing a thin finger at Matt. "He attacked us! We were on duty, you know!"

"Duty?" one of the women asked. "Drinkin' duty, corporal? The three of you felt fearful, did you? Frightened of a cripple and this stranger? Somebody get the sheriff! Quick!"

"Forget the sheriff," another argued. "Find a rope!"

The soldiers stumbled to their feet and fled down the street toward the fort. An angry collection of townsmen chased them until a squad of soldiers appeared, rifles in hand, to restore order.

"Nothin' more you can do, Cully," one of the saloon girls said, leading the boy away from the corpse. "He's finally at peace."

"Uncle Ab?" the youngster called.

"We'll see he's taken care of," a tall man dressed in farmer's overalls promised. "Maybe Fitz'll put you up for the night."

"I can tend my own self," Cully insisted, turning to Matt. "Thanks for what you did, Mr. Ramsey. Your gear's here, safe like I promised."

"Don't you worry 'bout that," Matt said, frowning. "Should've kept out of it, I'd say."

"Wasn't you, son," the farmer told Matt. "Ole Ab's been hurryin' to his death since that shell took his leg at Elkhorn Tavern. Fool way to get shot, though, dropped by a drunk Yankee and all."

"No real good way to die," a gruff voice declared.

Matt turned and beheld O. T. Fitzpatrick. The liveryman lifted Matt's saddle onto one shoulder and motioned for Cully to follow. Matt picked up his saddle blanket and the pile of belongings wrapped in the buffalo hide.

"You did fair tonight," Fitz commented as the farmer and another man carried the fallen captain toward the opposite side of the street. "What d'you say, Culver? He figure to be a man that'd be able to put up with an ole cuss like me?"

"Like as not bash your head, you sourball," the boy replied, wiping his eyes.

"I'm used to sleepin' out in the open," Matt said as he followed toward the livery. "Don't mind about me."

"You made enemies tonight," Fitz explained. "Not wise to be out o' doors. 'Sides, I thought you were lookin' for work."

"Am," Matt said.

"Well, I could use a pair o' hands just now. 'Course the work'll be hard, and I'm no bargain as a boss, am I, Culver? It'd be free board for your horse, though, food if you can stomach it, and five dollars every Friday you last."

"I won't get rich," Matt observed.

"None of us do," Fitz grumbled. "But if you don't mind smellin' Culver here, and the stock'll tolerate you, the job's yours."

"That mean I'm hired on, too?" Cully asked.

"You know Ina's been after me a month to get you from behind that barrel, boy!" Fitz said, swinging his free arm around to enclose the boy's slight shoulders. "Stable's not a mighty improvement, 'course, but now your uncle's . . ."

"Sure," Cully agreed, wrapping an arm around the liveryman's considerable girth. "Figure she'll have me in church, too?"

"And school as well now it's September," Fitz added. "But then a little schoolin' won't spoil you too much, I'd say."

"Next thing you know she'll be scrubbin' me with lye," Cully said, grinning.

For once, Matt thought, something good's come of death. The thought warmed him. But later, when he spread his blankets in the straw and snuffed the candle, he heard Cully's restless thrashing about. The boy whined and sniffled half the night until Matt finally fetched the buffalo hide and spread it atop the shivering youngster.

"Pa?" the boy called.

Matt started to offer a comforting word but thought better of it. He had his own brothers to tend, and Cully was better off sharing his fears with someone offering more permanent attention.

# CHAPTER

## ★ 13 ★

Matt rose with the sun that next morning. The straw beneath him failed to offer the same firm comforts of the slat bed and mattress back at the bunkhouse, and he rose stiff and sore. His jaw ached, and two notable bruises attested to his intervention at the saloon.

"Mornin'," Cully called from the horse stalls.

Matt turned in surprise, for the voice was oddly high and foreign. He recognized the youngster, returned the greeting, and set about pulling on a pair of trousers.

"They're buryin' Uncle Ab in a bit," Cully said. "It'd be nice to have some folks there. He was a soldier, you know. Not many hereabouts remember him, and some who do won't come. I hate to think he'll just be dropped in a hole and covered up with hardly a nod."

"I served the Southern cause myself," Matt said. "I'll come."

The boy offered no response, just dipped his chin slightly. Matt supposed it to be the hardest kind of loss, the death of a relative who had likely been a disappointment and embarrassment more often than anything else. And yet there was no mistaking Cully's feelings.

As Matt buttoned his shirt, Cully walked over and set the rolled buffalo hide beside the wall where Matt had laid the Sharps.

"Guess you misplaced that," Cully whispered.

"Sure," Matt agreed.

"Miz Ina's bakin' up some biscuits for us to eat," the boy said somberly as he stepped into a pair of boots that wouldn't properly fit for a good year and a half. "Eggs an' bacon, too. She cooks fair, you know. I been gettin' scraps off her for six weeks or so now."

"Well, there's a lot to be said for a job that feeds you well."

"You got money, though," Cully declared. "Shoot, you paid me for waterin' your horses when you could as easily put him by a trough. I'd bet you got brothers."

"House full of 'em, and nephews near as big as you, Cully."

"No wife yet?"

"Almost," Matt said, staring at his feet.

Cully recognized the sadness draining Matt's face and matched the frown. The two of them shared an unspoken word of consolation. Then the clanging of a spoon against a tin pan announced breakfast. Cully motioned toward the stable door, and Matt followed to where Ina Fitzpatrick had set a wash basin.

"I see so much as a smudge of dirt on face or hands, Culver, I swear I'll toss you in a tub and scrub you myself!" the woman called from the door.

"She'd do it, too," Cully declared. "Women always tryin' to peel a man's clothes off him, you know. Ma'am, you got amorous intentions?"

Matt turned and watched Ina Fitzpatrick grab a rolling pin and set after young Cully with a purpose. For a small woman of delicate features, Ina packed a wallop in her wrists. The pin soon landed on Cully's backside, and Matt kept clear while she tugged the boy by one ear to the basin and waved a cake of soap to his lips.

"Some may be used to such wild ways, Culver Herrick, but I'm not one of 'em," she scolded. "You'll get a Christian upbringin' from now on, and a Methodist hidin' if it's needed."

"Yes'm," Cully said, cowering in pretended fear when she

half-heartedly raised the rolling pin over his head. He then grinned at Matt. "Told you she was fond o' me," the boy added.

"Boys!" Ina grumbled as she returned to her quarters. "The devil's handiwork, every one of 'em!"

"She gets excited some, too," Cully pointed out. "Am I clean enough?"

Matt examined both hands and shook his head. Cully had barely made a dent in the accumulated grime. An hour's soaking in a hot tub wouldn't clear away the dust and dirt.

"At least get the mud from beneath your fingernails," Matt advised. "What's needed is a good bath."

"Bath?" the boy said nervously. "Mr. Ramsey, you know a man gets to smellin' o' lilac and lye, horses take to gettin' suspicious."

"Well, as things are now, a skunk's apt to mistake you for his long lost son," Matt countered. "We'll see if Miz Ina's got a tub she'll loan you."

"Bath's unhealthy. Everybody knows that."

"So's a whack on the rump with a rollin' pin," Matt pointed out.

Cully frowned and skipped away as Matt took the soap, but Matt applied the harsh lather to his own face and hands. He left the Fitzpatricks to worry over Cully.

The breakfast proved up to Cully's praise and more. Matt favored the taste of black pepper, but he hadn't sampled it in better than a year. The biscuits rivaled those of Devona Pickworth and clearly put Stump Riley's rock-hard concoctions to shame.

"That's the way I like to see a plate cleaned," Ina commented when Matt soaked up the last bit of egg yolk with a nub of biscuit. "Care for some more, young man?"

"Name's Matt," he told her. "Afraid I daren't, ma'am. I got to fit these trousers awhile yet."

"Well, I'd say you were safe on that account," she said, grinning. "Pure skeleton thin, you are. Bad as this boy, though filthy as he is, I don't guess we'll ever know. If I'd known 'bout your uncle earlier, Culver, I'd have had you in a tub. Folks ought to 'pear respectable at a buryin'."

"He'll do," Fitz said, clasping his wife's wrist. "Folks that'll be there know Culver already. Ain't his fault he's fallen on hard times. I'm not high on washin' myself, but then I don't put it off a year. We'll heat some water once chores're tended. That suit you, Culver?''

"It'd suit me better for you to call me Cully," the boy answered.

"Well, we can try that by and by," Fitz promised. "Can't say I know you much now, all coated with dust and grit."

"All right," Cully said, raising his hands in mock surrender. "I'll take a bath. Just you see that woman keeps her hands clear o' me. I wouldn't want to be the cause o' no trouble 'tween you and your wife, Fitz."

Ina raised both eyebrows, and her hand reached for the rolling pin. A grin stretched from one of devilish Culver Herrick's ears to the other. A brief howl of delight escaped his lips, and Ina collapsed in her chair in a fit of laughter. Fitz joined in, and for a few moments Matt even warmed. Then Cully recalled the burying. He grew quiet instantly, then gazed sadly out the window toward the churchyard back of the Methodist meeting house.

"You'll be there, won't you Fitz?" Cully asked. "Miz Ina?"

"We'll be with you," the woman assured him. "Reverend Potts plans to read some words of comfort, and Miz Devona and her girls'll sing a bit."

Cully brightened some. And when they walked together to the churchyard, his step quickened. A huddle of townspeople gathered beside the grave while three former comrades, dressed in Confederate gray, carried the fallen captain, wrapped in a quilt donated by one of the saloon girls.

Reverend Potts shared several verses, but Matt heard few of them. He wasn't high on funeral talk, and he'd've stayed at the livery if his being along hadn't seemed so important to young Cully. The singing was better, and the shared memories of the soldiers brought tears to others who had lost loved ones in the fighting.

Finally, Ina Fitzpatrick led Cully to the hole and showed him how to sprinkle a bit of dirt over the body. The boy did so, and others filed past somberly to do the same.

"We'll fill it in, Cully," one of the gray-clad men pledged. "Later on I'll get a marker carved."

"You'll put on it he was a cap'n?" Cully asked.

"And how he gave his best till he lost a leg," the soldier promised. "I'll leave out him bein' shot and such. The date's enough. No need for folks to know it all."

"Sure," Cully agreed.

With the day begun so soberly, Matt half expected a sour mood to hang over the stable. Instead Fitz handed over a pair of pitchforks and had his new employees shovelling dung half the morning. Later, fresh hay was spread out, and water troughs were emptied and refilled.

After a brief break for a midday dinner, Cully passed most of the afternoon exercising the horses while Matt helped Fitz salve a mare's injured tendon and replace a shoe thrown off by a wayward colt.

"You got a fine way with horses," Fitz observed as Matt combed burs out of the coat of a chestnut gelding. "Knew it first time I gazed at that big black. Powerful lot o' horse for a stablehand, Matt. Don't figure you'll last here long."

"Why's that?"

"Oh, I don't know exactly the way to put it. Way I see things, a horse like that won't give over his spirit to just anybody. He won't stand for bein' kept in a corral, you know. Lord meant that horse for the open plains, for some tall Kiowa chief or maybe a cavalry general. By and by you're bound to find somethin' better."

"Then why hire me on?" Matt asked.

"Well, for one thing, I like you some. You got a sense o' justice, and that suits me. Th'other thing's Culver's taken to you. Me an' Ina, we've raised a family and sent 'em out into the world. I got no easy manner with boys, and they need a bit o' that."

"Was you he went to last night," Matt reminded Fitz.

"But likely you supplied some comfort. I haven't found much in this life. I guess you could say you're here to break me to the task, gentle me some."

"Cully'll do that, Fitz."

"Sure, but you see, he'll need some breakin' in, too. Like that bath. You see me scrubbin' a youngster, Matt? I'd be more likely to peel off half his hide. Ina never let me near our kids till they could fend some for themselves. Once he's tamed some, I'll be able to handle the reins—better'n you would, I expect. Boy needs somethin' solid to lean against, and you'll be on your way in time."

"Got it all figured out?"

"So do you. I hear you had a brother not much older'n Culver ridin' with you a week back. You sent him somewhere solid, didn't you? There's sense to you, Matt Ramsey. And a bit o' wildness, too, I'd judge.''

Matt gazed at the liveryman with surprise. The old man read people well, didn't he? Just then Matt wasn't looking to head anywhere, though. He welcomed the work, the company, and the calm.

The latter didn't last till supper, though. An Indiana drummer named Dalton Kenway hired a sorrel mare to make his rounds.

''She's a gentle sort,'' Fitz explained to the man. ''An' if you get confused by the trails, Little Sally here knows the way home.''

The Indianan seemed pleased by the news, climbed atop the saddle, and rode out to the east. He returned the mare winded, well spent, thirsty, and lathered from rough use. When Matt complained of the ill treatment, Kenway tossed two silver dollars on the ground and laughed.

''I paid my money. It's for me to treat a horse as I see fit,'' the drummer declared.

''Lord, Matt, look at her flanks!'' Cully cried.

Matt gazed at the marks made by spurs. His face reddened as he approached the rider.

''Wasn't me,'' Kenway claimed. ''I wear no spurs.''

''You got 'em in your bag, though,'' Matt roared, tearing the sample bag from the man's hands and emptying its contents on the floor of the stable. Among the catalogues and sketches were a pair of Spanish spurs.

''I paid my money,'' Kenway repeated.

''You know there's just one thing I hate worse'n a man who hurts a horse,'' Matt said as fury rose in his eyes. ''That's a liar!''

The Indianan turned, but he failed to move quickly enough. Matt grasped Kenway by the shoulders, lifted him off the ground, and threw him into a pile of recently collected manure.

''Oh, Lord,'' Kenway whined as he tried to get to his feet. His clothes were stained hopelessly by the muck, and his face and hair were speckled with it as well.

''I'll see you fired!'' Kenway shouted, shaking his hat angrily.

''I see you about another minute, mister, I'll show you how a Texan uses those spurs o' yours!'' Matt replied.

Kenway scrambled to collect his samples. Matt glared when

the man reached toward the spurs, and they were left in the straw.

"There's another livery, you know," Kenway declared. "Wait till I spread the word Fitzpatrick's hired on a madman!"

"I'd watch my words if'n I was you," Cully advised. "He didn't get those bruises pitchin' drummers into dung heaps."

Kenway scurried away, raising a clenched fist. He met O. T. Fitzpatrick on his withdrawal and howled about the outrage.

"What'd you do to the fool, Matt?" Fitz asked moments later.

"He used these on the sorrel," Matt explained, handing over the spurs.

Fitzpatrick examined the horse angrily, then tossed the spurs against the stable wall.

"Yeah, I know the sort well enough," Fitz declared. "You can't drag 'em all through horse leavin's, though. It's their town now, Matt. Don't bruise so easy. You run off all my trade, we'll have to eat owl eggs and coon gizzards."

"Didn't know coons had gizzards," Matt said, grinning.

"That fellow earned what he got," Cully insisted. "Sally's cut bad, and she was near dried out from runnin' hard in this sun with no water."

"You got to rethink your notions 'bout justice," Fitz said, gazing somberly at each of his companions in turn. "Just last week a farmer got himself locked in jail 'cause he took offense at a soldier offerin' attentions to his daughter. Understand, that farmer didn't lay one hand on the bluecoat, just shouted some. It was enough."

"Can't be," Matt complained. "Isn't right."

"Is true, though," Fitz said, spitting the distaste from his mouth. "Justice is one thing, boys. Survivin's another."

Matt gave the warning considerable thought. After all, Fitz didn't seem the kind to back away from a thing without reason.

After supper they spoke a bit more of it. Then Ina hauled a wooden tub to the barn, and Matt set it in an unused stall. In half an hour, three buckets of water had been heated, and Matt pumped another two buckets of cool to temper the bath somewhat. Then, shielded by a wall of patchwork quilts, Culver Herrick stripped and plunged into the water.

"Still too hot, Matt," the youngster complained.

"Don't talk," Matt answered. "Get that brush to movin'. It

won't stay hot, and soon enough you'll be howlin' your tail end's frozen off.''

"Not this time o' year," Cully argued.

Matt shook his head and collected the soiled garments Cully had tossed over the wall of the stall.

"You can't get back into these," Matt grumbled, "and a good washin's bound to turn 'em to rags."

"I got no others," Cully explained. "Can't go naked, Matt."

"I'll see if Ina's maybe got somethin' put back from her kids."

Matt carried the threadbare garments into the house, and Ina pronounced them best fit for the stove. She committed them to the flames, then scrounged around in an old chest.

"Well, I don't suppose this'll do," she said, holding up a small dress.

"I wouldn't care to be scalped," Matt told her. "How 'bout a nightshirt, a pair o' drawers, somethin' he can sleep in. Tomorrow we can get him some overalls at the mercantile."

Ina searched high and low, but the best she could manage was a pair of her old bloomers. Matt took them in hand and set off reluctantly for the stable.

Matt expected open rebellion, but when he set the bloomers atop the quilt wall, Cully responded by throwing the scrub brush at Matt's head.

"Lord, Matt, get my clothes back. It's worse'n I thought. That woman's out to turn me into a girl!"

"Is not," Matt said, rescuing the brush and climbing the stall so as to face the fuming youngster. "It's just for you to sleep in. Tomorrow I'll fetch some overalls from the mercantile myself."

"Promise?"

"I promise," Matt said, shaking the straw from the brush and returning it to Cully's outstretched hand. "You got to give 'em a chance, you know. It's not just Fitz takin' you in to help with the horses. They mean for you to be family."

"I know," Cully said, gazing up at Matt with confusion. "I never had any practice bein' somebody's son, Matt. Uncle Ab took me when I was seven, and he mostly let me roam wild. I slept in empty barrels or out in the open, on the piano bench in a saloon or behind a bar. I don't know polite talk. I barely been 'round a woman in all my days, and I can't remember what the inside of a church is like. I can't read, Matt. They'll find out and want to be shed o' me."

"That's not how it works," Matt said, shaking his head. "You don't know these two. They've taken you to heart, Cully, made you a mission o' sorts. You couldn't shake 'em with a stick."

"I figured maybe I could ride out with you and hunt horses."

"Not many left hereabouts," Matt explained. "You been wild, Cully. Like it much?"

"Didn't have to take baths," the boy grumbled.

"Not doin' too good a job o' one now," Matt observed. "Got to scrub your back, Cully, get the dirt off. The front o' you's almost human now. The back—well, that skunk may still hunt you down."

"Ma used to scrub that for me."

"I'm nobody's ma," Matt reminded Cully. "I guess we could pay one o' those ladies down at Sudsville to wash you, but it seems a waste o' good money when you can do it yourself."

"Mattie Allen gave me a bath once," Cully said, grinning. "Mattie was particular fond o' Uncle Ab. She worked the Sundown Saloon till she shot ole Frank Johnson and had to leave town."

Cully's eyes rolled for a few minutes, then he started scrubbing vigorously. Shortly the grime began floating away.

"Now the hair," Matt said, nodding when Cully shook his head in rebellion. The boy dipped his head under the murky water, shook his hair so that soap bubbled about the stringy ends, then lathered up so that he appeared to be a sickly pink skeleton with a snowy mountain for a head.

"Brush it hard now," Matt advised. "Harder! Get it clean."

Cully labored at it hard, then rinsed the suds away. The water had, as predicted, begun to chill, and Cully called for a blanket. Matt tossed it to the youngster's eager hands, then left the boy to dry himself.

A few minutes later, Cully emerged wrapped in the blanket, a wrinkled prune of a boy.

"How's it feel to be clean again?" Matt asked.

"Human," Cully confessed, running his hands through stringy hair that had gone from charcoal black to light auburn. "I guess we couldn't find a barber this time o' night."

"No, but I've clipped my own hair for years, and I worked on half the company during the war."

"How many of 'em are bald now?"

"Oh, I do all right with the shears," Matt said, digging the clippers from his belongings. "Be glad you've a while 'fore you start shavin'. I sliced a few cheeks in my time."

"You'll cut it back so the girls won't laugh when Miz Ina takes me to the schoolhouse?"

"Do my best, peanut."

"Why'd you call me that?" Cully asked as Matt brushed back the boy's hair and began to trim away the excess.

"Oh, it's somethin' I used to call my brother Luke. Then Bucky. Others since. You look a bit like 'em just now."

"How so?"

"Hard to say exactly. Kind o' lost, and kind o' scared. But sure as the moon that you'll get to the end o' the road."

Cully grinned, and as Matt completed the transformation, the boy emerged as a rather pleasant-looking twelve-year-old, skinny but bright-eyed.

"I wish we could show you to Ina," Matt said, collecting the mountain of shed hair and raking it to one side of the stable.

"Not in that!" Cully cried, pointing to the bloomers.

"Well, you always said she favored you in the altogether."

"If I didn't like you, Matt Ramsey, I'd likely put a pitchfork in your blankets."

Matt laughed, then left the boy to rub the moisture from his body and climb into the bloomers. Matt spread out his blankets, shed his clothes, and climbed into bed, oddly content for once. The candle went out shortly, and Cully scrambled into his bedding on the opposite wall of the stable.

" 'Night, Matt," Cully called as he settled into the straw.

" 'Night, peanut," Matt answered.

There was less thrashing about that night, and the buffalo hide remained in its place beside the Sharps. As for Matt Ramsey, he dreamed of a little room in a small farmhouse a hundred miles east in Fannin County. He saw the shining eyes of brothers and nephews, sipped coffee with Amos and Rose Margaret. In the window he thought he caught a glimpse of a phantom Kate Silcox.

"Welcome home, Matt," they all seemed to say at once.

*Home?* he thought, blinking his eyes awake. *Where's that?* Sleep overwhelmed the question, though, and peace swept doubts to another place and time.

# CHAPTER
# ★ 14 ★

By breakfast, Matt had roused the mercantile owner, a grumpy fellow named Oates, and procured for Cully two pairs of overalls, three rough cotton workshirts, the appropriate undergarments, and a nightshirt to replace the bloomers. The boy all too gladly exchanged the oversized, muslin ''baggy'' for the new outfit. And if the clothes left considerable room for future growth, Matt assured him it wouldn't be long before Ina's cooking added the needed inches.

Washed, decked out in his new clothes, with hair clipped to a respectable length, Culver Herrick seemed a stranger. Matt marveled that such a transformation was possible. Cully seemed years younger, thin as a fencepost, suddenly more child than midget man.

Gazing in a bit of tin Matt carried for want of a mirror, Cully barely recognized himself. ''That me?'' he gasped.

''Guess so,'' Matt answered. ''Who else'd it be?''

Cully nodded as he rolled up the cuffs of the overalls so as not to trip while walking. He tugged at the blue straps that threatened to slide off his shoulders, touched the fabric of his shirt, and grinned broadly.

106

"They're sure to keep me, don't you figure?" Cully asked. "I'm mostly human again."

Matt nodded, then smoothed out a rebellious strand of auburn hair and marched Cully to the wash basin.

Fitz and Ina were struck by the change. It wasn't Fitz's way to extend flattery, but he couldn't help nodding approvingly.

"Looks like we ordered him out of some drummer's catalogue," the liveryman said, gazing at his wife.

Ina didn't bother with words. Instead she bounded over, drew Cully's back to her breast, and wrapped her arms around the boy's neck.

"You do us proud, Cully," she whispered.

"Told you she'd have her hands on me first chance," Cully said as she kissed his forehead. He made no effort to escape, though.

It warmed Matt to think he'd had a hand in setting something right, though he missed Cully's constant jabbering that morning in the stable. The boy set off with Fitz on horseback, leaving Matt to tend the chores alone.

The soldiers appeared an hour later. Matt didn't notice until Ina appeared in the stable door with Sergeant Ray Calvin. The woman's rare appearance amid the horses startled Matt more than the bluecoated sergeant's arrival, and he set aside the harness he was mending and turned their way.

"They come to talk to you," Ina said, her forehead wrinkling with concern.

"Best come along," the sergeant advised.

Outside, next to the corral, Colonel Washburn paced while a corporal's guard blocked all escape paths. At the officer's side was a bewhiskered gent Ina identified as the new federal judge, Morris Waxman. The hated corporal who had slain Ab Herrick stood with the dark-haired private beside the gate of the corral.

"That's him," the corporal said, pointing an accusing finger in Matt's direction.

"Yes, sir, he's the one," the private agreed.

"We've had trouble with this one before," the officer said, recalling their previous meeting. "Refused to sell us horses."

"That's not exactly right, judge," Matt objected.

"You'll hold your tongue, Reb!" the colonel ordered, nodding to Sergeant Calvin.

"Easy," the sergeant whispered as Matt took a step toward Washburn.

"Morris, you know we've got to put an end to this sort of thing," Washburn argued. "You'd agree these unrepentent rebels merit punishment. Attacking federal troops in the course of carrying out their duties amounts to an act against the state."

"Yes, sir," the corporal agreed. "Hang the fellow, judge! Young Boley's laid up a week at least with cracked ribs, and we two aren't fit for ridin'."

"This one did all that by himself?" the judge asked, raising an eyebrow.

"Judge," Ina broke in, "there's plenty o' witnesses saw what happened. If these two were doin' their duty, then I suppose that includes shootin' unarmed townfolk and drinkin' their gut full o' whiskey."

"The reb resisted federal authority," the colonel insisted.

"That brave one there," Ina said, pointing to the corporal, "shot down an unarmed veteran with but one leg. I'm sure he was a mighty threat to your authority, cap'n, as was the boy they set upon."

"I hold the rank of brevet colonel, madam," Washburn said, rolling the final word in such a way that it seemed to cast doubts on Ina's character. Matt's face reddened instantly.

"I heard about this unfortunate shooting," the judge said, turning toward the soldiers. "That was you who did it, eh, corporal? I understand you two took offense at the man's gray coat."

"Filthy rebs," the corporal said, sensing sympathy in the judge's words. "We fought 'em 'cross Georgia, you know, the backshootin' sons o' Satan. Now they attack us when we're doin' our best to keep wild Indians from scalpin' their women and kids! I say leave the whole o' Texas to dry up and blow away."

"And here I thought the war was over," Matt said, staring hatefully at the corporal. "I signed my parole papers, judge, and I don't hold your duties against you. Taxes are high, some say, but my family's always paid 'em. I fought two years, but I never held it against you fellows for takin' up arms, and you beat us fair enough at Vicksburg. Good men on both sides fell there."

"He's right," Sergeant Calvin said, nervously eyeing the colonel. "I buried friends, but those were good men fought on th'other side."

"Sergeant, what's come over you?" Washburn cried. "You fought under the Union banner! Forget what color that uniform is?"

"I ain't forgot a thing," the sergeant answered. "Or a man laid low. Those fellows put down their arms, though. It's time we had the anger behind us."

"Ought to run you for president," the officer said through gritted teeth. "Getting fair at making speeches. You might remember you're still in the army."

"Exactly what do you know of this matter, Calvin?" the judge asked.

"Not all that much," the sergeant confessed. "I recall meetin' Mr. Ramsey here before when we was lookin' for remounts. Colonel likely's confused him 'cause we seen so many horse traders lately. Mr. Ramsey was set to sell his stock to us, all right, but we, well, wanted to do some more lookin'."

"And the shooting?" Judge Waxman asked.

"Only heard 'bout that at the barracks," Sergeant Calvin said, turning to the corporal. "Do know the three of 'em was absent from their picket posts, and when they come in, was liquor on their breath. Had half the town chase 'em to the gate, too. I'd guess there were witnesses about like the lady here says."

"Plenty," Ina assured them.

"Judge, we got to start gettin' along, wouldn't you say?" Calvin asked. "Lot o' good men died to preserve our Union, not tear it apart for good. I don't see where Mr. Ramsey here did anything you or me wouldn't have done in his place. From the look of him, he didn't exactly get off scot free."

"Colonel Washburn?" Waxman asked.

"I've brought my charges," the officer insisted. "If need be, I can use my own authority to jail this man."

"Only the post commander can do that," the judge said sourly. "I don't think you'd want to bring this to him, George. Don't take me for a fool. I've got ears. There are folks in Jacksboro saying your corporal here's the one should hang. I won't have that, but I surely won't abide you adding wood to the flame! I'd say drunken on duty merits a tour in the guardhouse, and the rest is best forgotten. Ramsey?"

"I've got no quarrel with anybody," Matt declared.

"There's a boy's lost his uncle," Ina said, frowning.

"Appears he's found quarters," Waxman observed. "Or so I

hear. If that changes, or there's expense incurred, I'll set it right myself."

"We tend our own," Ina muttered.

"Then I believe we've settled our business here," Judge Waxman said, stretching his arms to his sides. "Haven't we, Colonel?"

Washburn gazed hatefully at Matt, then stalked off, waving the corporal's guard along. Sergeant Calvin escorted the two miscreants personally.

"Lot o' gall they got, comin' here that way," Ina remarked when the soldiers had departed.

"Thanks for speakin' up," Matt told her.

"Not everyone's lost their senses these days," she replied. "You watch out, though, Matt. That soldier fellow's got mean eyes, and he's got the eagles on his shoulders to do some real harm."

Matt nodded sadly, then resumed his duties.

If life had been just, then Washburn's exit should have marked the end to Matt's troubles. But no Ramsey had ever found an easy trail. Half a week later, just after Cully set off for his first day at the schoolhouse, two gentlemen in matching striped coats rode up on horseback and accosted Fitz.

"Name's Hank Jarvis," the taller of the two announced. "This is my brother Foley here. We've been lookin' to take on some new property in town. You know we've bought Ferguson's stable and the old Stewart livery outside town."

"Got a mercantile and the hotel," Foley added. "Got in mind to take on this place, too."

"It's not for sale," Fitz said, turning away.

"Oh, everything's for sale," Hank Jarvis argued. "Once the price is met. I'd say a hundred dollars'd be fair."

"A hundred dollars wouldn't buy the stock," Fitz said, laughing. "A thousand dollars wouldn't change my mind, either. I got a good business, and I aim to hold on to her."

"I can be persuasive," Foley said, grinning at his brother.

"Good day," Fitz barked.

"He doesn't understand, does he, Hank?" Foley added. "Folks generally come around to our way o' thinkin'."

"Sure, Fitzpatrick," Hank declared. "You could have yourself a fire. That kid you've taken in could fall down a well. Somebody could get shot . . . by accident."

"Accident?" Matt asked, reaching behind a stack of hay and pulling out his Colt. "Funny thing 'bout accidents. I don't much believe in 'em."

"Who's he?" Hank asked his brother.

"The man who'll settle with you should any accident happen to Fitz or his livery," Matt growled, turning the pistol on the brothers. "Matt Ramsey. You ask around some. You'll find out I got my own talent for persuasion."

"Old man, you're bargainin' for hard times," Foley threatened.

Fitz grabbed a pitchfork and started for the brothers. Hank reached for a pistol, but Matt rammed the hammer back on his Colt, and Hank froze.

"Git!" Fitz yelled.

"Or stay," Matt said, stepping to within an inch of Hank Jarvis's face. "I haven't peeled a big-mouthed fool in months! Well?"

The Jarvis brothers backed their way toward the street. Neither seemed quite to know what to say. In the end, they said nothing, just angrily marched off.

"There's trouble, Matt," Fitz observed. "You know, son, you're makin' a fair share o' enemies these days."

"Always had a way with folks," Matt said, grinning.

"I've heard about those Jarvis boys," Fitz added, frowning as he scanned the street. "Little Billy Stewart got his leg broke, and the Fergusons had their feed poisoned."

"We'll have to be careful," Matt declared. "I meant what I said, too, Fitz. We have trouble, I'll be visitin' those fellows."

"I know, Matt. So do they. If I was you, I'd watch the shadows, my friend. And I'd sit with my back to the wall."

Two nights hence, Matt was awakened from a deep sleep by the sound of the big black whinnying in the corral outside. Matt instinctively rose to his feet and collected his pistols.

"Somebody's out there," Cully observed as he cautiously made his way, ghostlike in his white nightshirt, toward the door.

Matt dressed hurriedly, then set off to investigate. Three shadows lurked beside the corral. One doused a stack of hay with coal oil, and another prepared to set it alight.

"Matt?" Cully whispered as he crept over.

"What's that?" Hank Jarvis called, turning toward the flash of white. The figure holding the torch drew a pistol and turned toward the stable. Matt pushed Cully to the ground, covered the boy's squirming body with his own, and opened fire.

The newspaper described it afterward as a battle. It wasn't. Matt had seen battles, and what followed was over almost before it had begun. The Colt barked four times, felling Hank Jarvis first and dropping the torchman second. The third figure fled toward the street, only to be blasted by O. T. Fitzpatrick's shotgun.

Matt leaped forward then and raced to where the torch was igniting the grass beside the corral. He stomped out the flames, then held the torch over the fallen raiders.

"Guess those boys made their last buy," Fitz grumbled, dragging the bloody corpse of Foley Jarvis from the street. Matt nudged the other bodies with his toe, was satisfied that death had rid the community of two scoundrels, then turned toward a shaken Cully Herrick.

The boy nestled under one of Ina's trembling arms, his pencil-thin legs and bare feet protruding eerily from beneath the nightshirt.

Soon candles lit windows in the adjoining buildings, and townspeople hurried to satisfy their curiosity. The sheriff arrived with Judge Waxman a half-hour later. Both men nodded as Fitz related the tale. The coal oil supported the story, and Waxman ordered the bodies dragged to the undertaker.

"Can't seem to keep from jumping into trouble, can you, Ramsey?" the judge asked.

"I seem to draw it to me," Matt said, sighing.

"Poor practice, young man. I'd consider finding another place to live if I was you. This keeps up, I'm afraid we'll wind up burying you . . . more than likely after stretching your neck some."

Matt frowned at the thought. Cully trotted over then and conducted him back to the stable. Matt kicked off his boots, shed his clothes, and collapsed in the straw. Cully then unwrapped the buffalo hide and stretched it over Matt's chest.

"Wasn't anything else you could do," the boy whispered. "They'd have burned us out certain."

"Sure," Matt muttered.

*It was true,* Matt admitted. He could have acted no differently. Nothing else could have been done. But as he turned on his side and prayed slumber would snatch him away, he knew excuses never made stomaching a killing any easier. Death once again had returned to cast its ugly shadow across Matt Ramsey's path. A world that only days before had appeared bright and inviting soured with each passing moment.

*I could leave*, Matt thought. *Climb atop the big black and ride.*

But where would he go that death couldn't find him?

# CHAPTER

## ★ 15 ★

For two days and nights Matt brooded. Except for taking meals with the Fitzpatricks and aiding Cully with his letters, Matt never left the confines of the stable. The big black grew restless and pranced anxiously around the corral, hoping Matt would slide back the rails and take to the plains again. But Matt had not the heart for riding . . . or anything else.

He might have remained in his stupor had not a surprise visitor appeared. Eli Lyttel sauntered through the stable's open door a little past noon and greeted Matt with a firm handshake.

"You're lookin' fit enough," Matt observed, examining the young man's leathery arms and tanned face. "Work suits you, it appears."

"Ranch chores keep a man occupied," Eli admitted. "Shovelin' hay does, too, I suppose. Rather be chasin' down mustangs, if you want to know the truth. And you, Matt?"

"I pass the time all right. Autumn's in the air now, and I don't look forward to a winter in the open. It's warm enough here, and Ina sets a fine table."

"Ought to. I hear you saved the place."

"Shot a couple o' fellows tried to set the corral alight. Fitz killed the other one."

"Still got that bad habit o' takin' on other folks' troubles, don't you, Matt?"

"Can't seem to get shed of it," Matt confessed, matching Eli's stern frown. "Hard to tell where their worries end and mine begin."

"Hear the sheriff's got his eyes on you now."

"Might be," Matt said, laughing nervously. "They got a Yankee judge here likes to talk about hangin' fellows."

"Hate to think o' you gettin' hung for lookin' out for somebody else," Eli muttered. " 'Specially when I know of a place where a man like you could get put to good use."

"Oh? That fellow Moss have trouble?"

"Somebody else," Eli explained. "There's a stage outfit set up west o' here, at a place called Trinity Crossin'. Old way station that was there got burned so often they quit comin' that route. Now, with all the new settlers, a stage line's needed. We got a stationhouse, barn . . ."

"We?" Matt asked.

"I hired on last week, Matt. Truth is, I hoped maybe you'd do the same."

"I got a job."

"Pay'd be better, and the work wouldn't be so much. Just tendin' horses and such. I wired Luke, and Gil's already signed on."

"Why hire four men to tend stock?" Matt asked.

"Well, they've had a run o' bad luck. Mainly Indian trouble. That's in our favor. Leaves us enough free hands to run down a few ponies."

"Any left?"

"Lots out that way," Eli replied enthusiastically. "Ought to see 'em, Matt, sturdy pintos and long, sleek brown racers like your black. Fine animals just waitin' for a man to throw a rope over 'em."

"It'd mean some fightin'?"

"Might," Eli confessed.

"I don't know that I've got the heart for fightin' anymore."

"From what I hear, you haven't done much else since hittin' town. Come on, Matt. We need a big brother around to keep us youngsters out o' trouble."

"Been a long time since you needed me, Eli," Matt argued. "You boys got your growth now."

"Never hurts to have a steady man callin' the hand, and none of us's done much business with Indians."

"I owe Fitz some time," Matt explained. "He's been good. There's a boy here, too, that's taken me to heart."

"You're not goin' to China, for God's sake. They won't hold you. Debts work both ways, Matt. Say your good-byes and ride out with me. You won't be sorry."

Matt walked outside. The stallion snorted and stomped its feet, and Eli laughed.

"He knows, don't you fellow?" Eli asked. "He's ready to ride right now."

"Isn't that easy," Matt said, kicking a rock across the clearing back of the livery.

"Sure it is," Eli said, motioning to where Fitz and Ina stood beside the pump. Matt knew Eli had already spoken to them.

"You'll want to wait for Culver to get back from his lessons," Fitz said, stepping over and gripping Matt's hands.

"I'll pack some food to speed you on your way," Ina said, rubbing a tear from her eye as she rushed to the door.

"It's for the best, you know," Fitz told Matt. "I told you before that you'd ride off by and by. We'll miss you some, I judge, but I suspect the way this beanpole of a friend o' yours talks, you'll have some ponies to sell me in time."

Matt nodded sadly. Ina then appeared with a flour sack of food. Matt took it, and she hugged his neck.

"God bless you, Matthew," the woman whispered to him. "You put a glow in this old place."

"That was Cully," Matt objected.

"There was no brightness to that boy till you shined him up," she explained.

"You get all your good-byes said," Eli suggested. "I'll meet you at the mercantile when you're ready. I got a list o' things to fetch."

Matt nodded his understanding, then set off to the stable to gather his belongings.

He had the big black saddled and waiting, with his bundled belongings tied across the horse's back, when Cully appeared.

"Got all the way to 'G' now," the boy announced proudly as

he raced over beside Matt. The boy's smile fell when he observed the Sharps tied behind the saddle.

"It's good you know your 'G's'," Matt said, reaching out and drawing the boy close. "Good-bye begins with a 'G.' "

Matt was surprised to discover his eyes had grown moist. It was rare for him to betray his feelings like that. Cully then wrapped both arms around Matt's hips, and Matt responded by resting a hand on the youngster's back. The two of them shuddered from the same shared feeling.

"Goin' far?" Cully asked.

"Trinity Crossin', they call the place. Stage station west o' here."

"They got Indians out that way, I hear. Best you stay here so I can watch out for you."

Matt grinned, and Cully held on tightly as if to hold him in place.

"Got to go now, peanut," Matt said, lifting the boy to the top rail of the corral.

"We need you here, Matt. There's lots o' work to do, and you got to . . ."

"You folks'll make out fine," Matt assured the youngster.

"I need you to . . ."

"You got Fitz and Ina for what's needed," Matt countered. "Cully, I gave what I had to give you. They've got what you need now."

"I'll miss you," Cully whispered.

"You'd better," Matt said, lifting the youngster's chin. "I'll expect a visit, and later on, a letter maybe. You work hard on those studies, hear? And don't give Ina too much of a battle next hair-clippin' time."

"I won't," Cully promised.

Matt was half tempted to throw the boy behind him on the horse and ride around the livery a few times, but that wouldn't make riding out any easier. Matt knew. He'd said good-byes before to brothers. That, after all, was what Culver Herrick had become.

Matt nudged the stallion into a slow trot and waved a final farewell, first to Cully and then to the Fitzpatricks. Soon he was riding down the street.

Eli was waiting as promised at the mercantile. It took but a moment for the younger man to climb atop his horse and lead the way north up the Buffalo Springs road. Soon, though, they swung west along a trail cut through the buffalo grass by iron-rimmed wheels.

The first ten miles neither rider spoke much. Then, as the trail reached the Trinity, Eli began describing the new farms sprouting up on both banks of the river.

"Not much up by the crossin', though," Eli admitted. "Guess that's why the Indians favor the place with their attentions."

"That'd seem likely," Matt agreed.

Just ahead, near a bend where the river deepened, a trio of barebacked farmboys dipped fishing lines in the water beneath the shade of a sprawling white oak. Eli waved, and the boys responded with like gestures.

"I remember how we all used to fish the creek back home," Eli declared, laughing merrily. " 'Course by and by you or Kyle was apt to toss us in, clothes and all."

"At least you had your clothes," Matt reminded Eli. "I recall the time you and Luke stole every stitch the Willis girls brought with 'em when they came down to take their bath."

"That was a picture, wasn't it?" Eli cried. "The two of 'em, prancin' homeward with yucca leaves to preserve their modesty."

"And you linin' half the county under fourteen up to watch from the bluff," Matt added.

The story kept them amused for better than an hour. Then, as they descended a series of hills overlooking the south bank of the Trinity, Matt motioned for silence.

"That where your station'd be?" Matt asked, pointing an anxious finger ahead to where a narrow column of smoke rose skyward.

"Close enough," Eli said, concern flooding his eyes.

"Best you leave me to lead the way awhile then," Matt said, sliding the Sharps from behind his saddle, loading the powerful rifle and then cautiously leading the way onward.

It wasn't long before Matt could sniff the scent of burning cedar and oak. A wail seemed to ride the wind, and pistol shots punctuated the air. Near the crossing itself, a derelict stagecoach stood on the open ground. The horses wandered aimlessly, still bound by harnesses that had been cut loose from the coach itself. Hogs rooted about on the far bank.

Matt signalled Eli to stop, then slid from the saddle. They

carefully tethered their horses in a cedar grove, then approached the crossing with care. Two mounted Indians watched as several companions exchanged shots with the stationhouse. The barn was half consumed by flame and smoke.

"Look," Eli whispered, pointing to the coach where a young Kiowa stripped the clothing from a stricken driver. Eli aimed his rifle, but Matt lifted the barrel.

"It's just a boy, Eli," Matt whispered. "Aim wide. We don't want the whole tribe down on us."

Eli clearly didn't understand, but he nevertheless followed Matt's instructions. It had always proven good practice in the past.

"Now," Matt said, and Eli fired his rifle toward the back of the coach. Instantly Matt raised an unearthly howl and started for the crossing, firing the Sharps toward the horsemen and then opening up with a pistol as he raced toward the stationhouse.

It was a crazed kind of a charge, and when Eli followed, screaming like a banshee, the Kiowas were unsettled. The Indians fought to control their startled horses, allowing Matt and Eli to splash through the shallows and race on toward the house. Those Kiowas engaging the building were threatened from behind . . . apparently by devils expectorated from the darker regions. The Indians ran toward their waiting horses, mounted in a flash, and rode off to the safety of the nearby wood.

Eli was the first to reach the door. Matt followed, coughing as he fought to catch his breath.

"Never was so glad to see anybody in all my life!" Gil Coleridge cried, embracing his friends. "Lord, we figured it was up for us."

Matt nodded, handed over his Sharps, and examined the retreating Kiowas.

"This here's Ben Hunter, Matt," Eli said, leading Matt to a weary man of perhaps forty years.

"You must be Ramsey," Hunter said, shaking Matt's hand. "I'm the fool they talked into being stationmaster o' this accursed place."

Hunter then introduced his wife, Flora.

"Thank you, sir," Mrs. Hunter said, clasping Matt's hand warmly.

"Flora, maybe you'd care to put a pot o' coffee on the stove?" Hunter asked.

"And get dinner started," she added. "You'll tend to the other?"

Hunter nodded, then pointed to a slender-shouldered figure slumped against the front window.

"I'll bring over the horses," Gil offered. "Driver's over there someplace, too."

"I'll give you a hand," Eli said, joining Gil.

While the two young men headed to the river, Matt stepped out onto the porch and kept watch for lingering Kiowas. They were well gone, though. Hunter located a spade and headed for a small rise overlooking the river. Two simple white crosses already marked the spot. The stationmaster started digging fresh graves.

Matt walked to the shambles of the barn, satisfied himself the fire would not spread, and returned to the house. Two women, a badly-shaken drummer, and an odd assortment of children huddled together on the porch. Matt thought to offer comfort, but what good were words when terror lurked so close?

There were, in all, four killed by the raiders—the driver, one of the women's husbands, the boy at the window, and a young stablehand named Leyland who'd been caught fetching water at the river and cut down. Ben Hunter dug trenches for each, and Eli cut the names of the slain in white pickets crossed to form markers. Leyland and the driver were cut up a good deal, and Hunter ordered them covered with canvas so as to avoid outraging the sensibilities of the passengers. Horace Wallace was given over to his family for a final farewell. The youngster in the window, thought to belong to one family or the other, was found instead to be one Toby Fowler, unknown to all except by the letters stitched in the lining of his coat.

"I'll jot down the circumstances of his death so anyone meeting the stage up the line will know what became of him," Hunter pledged. "Now, I think it's time we get on with the burying."

No one said much as the bodies were placed in the ground and quietly covered. Rosalie Wallace read a verse from her husband's Bible, and Eli led the singing of a favorite hymn. The children whimpered and clung to their mothers while the dazed drummer spoke of the fine new broad-brimmed hats his employer offered at surprising value.

It wasn't until the aroma of Flora Hunter's stew tempted their senses that the passengers began to revive. Bubbling kettles of beef with carrots and onions mixed in with potatoes and wild turnips brought back a hint of civilization somehow. Matt observed that only the salesman and the station crew emptied their plates, but then grief, after all, was as natural a thing as birth.

That night as the wind whistled through the trees, an old barn owl, likely dispossessed of his roost, hooted eerily from the treetops. The sound unsettled the children who soon whined and whimpered so that the whole station threatened to explode with suffering. Flora did her best to appease the youngsters with gingerbread and apple slices, but it was for naught.

"What's all this noise about?" Matt asked, crawling over among the little ones. Some hid behind blankets while others cowered against the wall and wailed fearfully. "You don't mean to tell me you're fearful of an old owl, do you?" The small heads nodded, and Matt grinned broadly. "Why, don't you know the thing to fear out west is the horned toad?"

"Is not," a boy of eight declared, dropping his blanket and resting his hands on his hips. "I seen plenty, and they're not scary at all!"

"Well, you don't know the half of it," Matt said, lifting his shirt. The old scars left by a Yankee saber met the curious eyes of the children. One girl lit a candle, and the boy ran his fingers along the pinkish line that marked Matt's belly.

"A toad did that?" the boy asked.

"Giant horned toad," Matt explained. He then launched a yarn about a menacing toad grown fat on gingerbread and lemonade. The toad swept across the state, spreading panic in its wake and devouring whole towns.

"Will it come here?" a girl asked nervously.

"Depends," Matt answered. "There any gingerbread and lemonade about?"

"Lots," Flora called from the far side of the room. "I thought for sure these children'd gobble it all up. Now I guess that toad'll be by for sure."

"Nooo," the children said, shaking their heads in disbelief.

"Toads don't eat gingerbread," the doubting boy complained.

"This 'un does," Matt insisted. " 'Course, if there wasn't any around, that toad'd likely look elsewhere."

The little ones exchanged anxious looks, then scurried to the table where Flora again spread out the treats. In no time the last crumb was devoured. The children, somehow set at ease by the

food, hurried back to their beds and fell into an uneasy sleep—
all but the boy, who sat for a time at Matt's side arguing that
toads have no taste for sweets.

"Guess I'll just have to prove it by havin' Miz Flora cook up
some more gingerbread," Matt finally said.

"No, she's tired," the boy said, his confidence shaking.

"Me, too," Matt said, lifting the boy and carrying him over
beside his teary-eyed mother. " 'Night, peanut.''

" 'Night, mister," the boy said.

Before Matt could escape, small hands reached out and
touched his departing shoulders. A little later Rosalie Wallace
led him aside.

"Thank you, Mr. Ramsey," she said, resting her head against
his tired shoulder. "They've a long journey tomorrow that you've
made easier."

"I lost a pa, too," Matt explained. "I know boys, you see.
I've got brothers."

"Bless you, sir, for driving off the heathens and easing our
pain."

"It's you needs the blessing, ma'am," Matt declared. "And
the sleep, too."

She nodded and retreated to the other side of the room. Matt
remained beside the window, staring off at the bright moon hovering overhead. He barely heard Eli Lyttel settle in alongside.

"Ever miss home?" the eighteen-year-old asked.

"Sometimes," Matt confessed. "Not the place, mind you.
The people. 'Course, Ma and Pa are gone, and Kyle's gone off
into the mountains."

"Luke'll be along. I sent him a wire."

"Be good to have his company."

"Yes," Eli said, nodding sadly. "I try to think of home, too,
sometimes, only I usually wind up rememberin' how we were
locked up in the jailhouse while Pa was on trial. He'd never have
gone so easy if they hadn't threatened to hang us, too. What is
it makes some folks so ugly mean, Matt? You see how those
Indians cut up poor Maury Leyland?"

"It's anger, partly," Matt supposed. "And feelin' they're in
the right. They were here first, you know, and they're fightin' to
hold onto their old ways. That's all over, o' course, and they're
finished, too."

"They don't seem to know it."

"Sure they do," Matt argued. "It's why you only see the old men and the kids. The old ones don't have anything left to lose, and the young ones, well, they're full o' dreams and adventure. It was the same at Vicksburg. In the end, the smart ones'll give it up, take to the reservations up in the Nations."

"And the rest?"

"We'll bury 'em," Matt declared. "Till they're all gone. Bound to be, Eli. Bound to be."

# CHAPTER

## ★ 16 ★

Matt, Eli, and Gil spent the better part of that next morning collecting the livestock, repairing the stagecoach, and restoring some semblance of order to the station. Twice, lone Kiowas appeared on the southern bank of the river, howling and waving lances in disdain of their besieged enemies.

"It's a good sign," Matt assured the frightened passengers. "All that yellin' means they aren't comin' callin' anytime soon."

"Maybe," the little Wallace boy suggested, "we ought to send 'em some gingerbread and lemonade. That way your ole horned toad can stomp on 'em for us."

"Why don't you ask Flora to mix some up?" Matt asked, grinning. "Then you can take it over there to that Indian yourself."

The boy scowled, and Matt promised himself to find a better tale if the children stayed a second night. Somehow the horned toad yarn lost some of its magic in the daylight hours.

Toward late afternoon, Ben Hunter satisfied himself that the wheels were sound, and Eli hitched a team to the coach. Gil was selected to drive the monster on to Jacksboro, where another driver could no doubt be hired.

"Don't forget to send those wires, too," Hunter reminded the young driver. "We need the lumber, not to mention another relief team."

"I got it all written down, boss," Gil said, patting his pocket. "Long as I don't attract any arrows, I'll get 'em sent."

As it turned out, Gil's debut as stage driver and telegram messenger proved uneventful, and he was back at Trinity Crossing early the following morning. A week thereafter three wagons hauled pine planks cut at a Tyler sawmill to the station, and work began on a new barn.

Except for taking time out to tend the livestock and exchange teams for the twice-weekly coaches heading east and west, Matt and the others spent every waking moment framing the new structure and then hammering planks into their proper places. The work was half completed when a sandy-haired rider appeared.

"It's Luke!" Eli called, abandoning his hammer as he rushed to greet his old friend. Matt merely waved to his brother and kept working. Luke refused to be met in so brusque a manner, though, and rode immediately past the stationhouse and bellowed out to his older brother.

"Thought you were hired to chase down horses and fight Indians!" Luke cried. "Now I find you're a carpenter. Somebody's gone and hired the wrong Ramsey for certain. Matt's the one never could put two boards side by side without one bein' crooked."

"So get off your horse and lend a hand!" Matt replied. "Use some o' that energy that's flappin' your jaw to do somethin' worthwhile."

Luke dismounted, tied off his horse, shed his shirt, and eagerly joined in the work. A great smile covered his face, and in no time the younger workers struck up a bawdy refrain.

"Run across any trouble on the trail west?" Matt asked Luke when the final verse concluded.

"Trouble? Didn't get scalped, if that's what you mean. Trouble? Only trouble was gettin' away without Bucky. Harvest time's not the best season on a farm, you know. He like to twist my arm off tryin' to talk me into comin'."

"Should've brought him," Eli suggested. "He's got a way o' raisin' spirits."

"Well, I thought some on it," Luke admitted, "but, well, I

figured if things settled down some, he could come later. There's no school out here, you know, and Ma always set great store by learnin'. And I knew Matt wouldn't need an extra worry.''

''Or an extra brother,'' Hunter said, chuckling to himself. ''Three would seem enough.''

Matt laughed, then resumed his labor.

The new barn rose gradually from the ashes of the old. Pine planks fleshed out the skeleton framework, and in a week Matt began constructing stalls for the horses. Gil cut post oaks for the corral poles while Eli and Luke finished shingling the roof.

It was an eastbound stage that first saw the finished barn. The driver, a tall, thin, tobacco-chewing Georgian named Ted Blanks, jumped down from the stage and swung the door open for his passengers.

Matt smiled as a shy girl of perhaps seven hid behind her mother's skirts. A boy slightly older darted out and made a run for the privy. The final two passengers were short, balding fellows most likely merchants. Their dour faces hinted they had not met with success farther west.

Eli and Luke changed the teams. They'd gotten rather good at it, and their quick hands and lively feet made short order of the task. Gil soaked a rag and did his best to erase the accumulated dust from the passengers' compartment. Flora Hunter, meanwhile, offered coffee and cakes to the weary travelers.

''Saw some Comanches twenty miles or so back up the trail,'' Blanks told Hunter when the passengers were all occupied inside the stationhouse. ''This keeps up, might be wise to mount a guard.''

''I mentioned it in my last report,'' Hunter said. ''You run across trouble up ahead, turn back. We've got good cover here and plenty of rifles.''

''Well, you can take it as gospel I won't be tryin' to outrun any Comanches with this rig!''

''We got Kiowas here lately,'' Hunter explained.

''Nor them either. I see you got the barn back up. They'll like as not burn this one as well. Fool soldiers ought to chase 'em to Canada, but they stay too busy playin' cards and gamblin' away their wages. And the drinkin'! Lord, these Yankees must have more corn liquor than blood in their veins.''

The Georgian began relating some of his experiences on the Llano, and his passengers gathered to listen. Ben Hunter opened his watch, frowned, and insisted the coach keep to its schedule. Flora handed over a tin plate of beef and beans, and Blanks hurriedly forked it into his mouth. Then, with passengers squeezed into their narrow quarters, the driver released his brake and set the fresh horses into motion.

The coach splashed through the river and rolled onward, leaving a dust trail to mark its path. Then, scarcely minutes after passing from view, the coach thundered back up the trail. This time, a band of bare-chested Indians raced alongside, firing arrows into the coach and howling like devils.

Matt raced inside the stationhouse, drew out his Sharps, and aimed at the closest Indian, still a hundred fifty yards away. The rifle boomed, and the warrior was blasted from his saddle. Other rifles began to crack out their welcome, too, and the coach soon lost its mounted tail.

In a matter of minutes, the accurate rifles emptied three saddles, allowing the coach to splash on to safety. While his companions rushed to tend the coach, Matt kept watch on the crossing. Young Kiowas collected their fallen comrades and shouted defiantly at the single rifleman now standing on the north bank of the river.

Then One Eye appeared. The scarred face of the Indian was painted with anger, and he prepared to send his warriors in a desperate charge against the station.

"No!" Matt called, waving his Sharps. "It'll be death, muerte!"

A trace of recognition crossed the Indian's brow, and he nodded grimly. For another minute Matt struggled to determine whether the Kiowas would charge or not. Finally, though, with their wounded slumped across horses, the Indians retired.

Matt, in turn, wheeled and marched back to the stationhouse. The back of the coach was full of arrows, and the doors held others. One of the merchants lay on the porch, an arrow protruding from his collarbone. Flora knelt beside the boy. An arrow had cut its way into the youngster's thigh, and she struggled to retard the bleeding.

"Goin' to lose that leg, son," Blanks muttered grimly.

"Nonsense!" Flora barked. "Ben, you pour out some o' that tea water and heat an iron. Once I dig out the barb, we'll stop the bleeding."

"Ever cut one out?" Matt asked Flora as he pulled Blanks away from the coach and gazed down at the youthful victim.

"You?" she asked.

"Get me a knife," Matt said, tearing a strip from his shirt. "We'll get the bleedin' stopped right now."

Matt had seen tourniquets applied aplenty while campaigning in Mississippi. Since returning home, he'd applied them twice. He repeated the process now, using a small twig to twist the cloth until the blood ceased to flow.

"Hurts some, eh?" Matt asked.

The boy whimpered something, then howled as Matt snapped off the end of the arrow shaft.

"Likely stopped when it struck bone," Matt told the boy's mother.

"Fine thing," she said, gripping her son's hand. "I thought they'd be safer in Waco with my mother. Who'd have thought this would happen?"

"No one," Matt told her as he lifted the boy from the bloody compartment and carried him around the coach and along to the house.

Flora Hunter might not have cut an arrow from anyone, but she understood what was needed. Already she'd cleared a table, was boiling strips of cloth, and had the necessary knives ready. Matt looked at the boy, grabbed a bottle from the bar, and handed it over.

"Drink some, son," Matt urged. "Some more," he added as the boy sipped the spirits.

"I don't hold with liquor," the mother said.

"I could give him a whack to the head, if you'd rather." Matt replied. "He kicks out while I got that knife in there, he *will* lose the leg, and that's for certain. You don't want to imagine what it'll feel like then, ma'am."

She nodded, and Matt tipped the bottle, allowing a bit more of the liquor to make its way into the youngster's gullet. The boy's eyes began to haze over, and he slurred his speech. Matt cut the boy's left trouser leg, then probed the reddened flesh to insure the alcohol had dulled the nerves sufficiently. It hadn't. The boy's face flashed white, and he ground his teeth. Matt took a deep breath and slid the knife along the length of the arrow shaft, found the head, then dug it out. Blood soaked the table and stained the floor, but Matt at last dislodged the arrow. He withdrew it slowly, patiently, then asked for the branding iron Flora had placed in the stove.

"Lord, what are you going to do?" the boy's mother cried.

"Sear the flesh," Matt explained, opening a powder cartridge and sprinkling the powder over the open wound. He then placed the hot iron against the flesh, allowing the sulfurous flash to cauterize the wound.

Drunk or not, the boy reacted to the blazing heat, issuing a solitary, piercing scream. Matt lifted the brand, and the boy fainted.

Matt stepped away and wiped the sweat from his face. Flora then hurried to wash the blood away and bind the jagged tear in the young thigh. Then and only then did Matt ease the tourniquet.

"Lord, help this child mend," Flora prayed.

"Ready for the next customer, Doc?" the wounded merchant called. Matt waved the man in, handed over the bottle, and prepared to cut the arrow from the man's collarbone.

Ted Blanks made a second, more successful, effort to guide his coach safely to Jacksboro later that afternoon. The two merchants, one still faint from loss of blood, accompanied bags of mail and assorted freight. The woman, who introduced herself as Mary Peterson, remained behind with her children, the three of them sharing one of the side rooms where Flora Hunter lodged overnight visitors.

Matt rode out twice to scout the trails for Kiowas, but One Eye had apparently vanished once more. Thereafter Matt busied himself chopping stove wood.

"You done a good job of it," Luke said, reading his brother's sour frown. "Must be hard, cuttin' into a body like that. Hard as fightin'."

"Harder," Matt grumbled. "I been in lots o' scraps."

"I know," Luke muttered.

"No, you don't know," Matt said, sending the ax slicing through a log three inches thick. "Wish to heaven I didn't."

"Matt?"

"Clouds a man's life, killin'," Matt said, discarding the ax and staring at his brother with eyes that bristled with sorrow.

"Tell me," Luke pleaded.

Matt related the clash with the Clancys, told of Ab Herrick's death, described the nightmare encounter with the Jarvis brothers at the livery.

"Before that there was the war," Matt added. "And the hard times back home. Seems sometimes I been fightin' and killin' my whole entire life, Luke. I've grown weary of it."

"Wasn't all bad times," Luke declared, reminding Matt of more cheerful days spent splashing away the summer or stalking deer in the autumn thickets. There were barn dances and pranks aplenty, but they only raised momentary smiles on Matt's face.

That night they spread their blankets in the barn. Matt felt a need to be alone, but Luke couldn't be shaken. Toward midnight a phantom face appeared in Matt's dreams, a smooth, creamy image pierced by the brightest eyes imaginable. Delicate pink lips parted, forming gentle, soothing words.

"It's all right, Matt," Kate Silcox told him. He could almost feel her touch, taste the sweet perfume of her cheeks. He whispered her name, reached out for her. But he grasped only emptiness, and the ghost sadly bid farewell.

"Kate!" Matt called out. "Kate, don't leave me!"

Matt felt something shaking him and blinked his eyes to chase away the shadowy haze that was taking possession of his senses. He saw Luke, recognized the barn, returned to the present.

"I saw her," Matt explained.

"It was a dream," Luke declared. "I have 'em, too."

"It was so real!"

"Yeah, I know," Luke said, easing his brother's troubled shoulders back into the straw. "I been thinkin' lately we been too long without some amusement, Matt. Eli was tellin' me they got these girls down in Sudsville that'll flat take your mind off your troubles forever. Maybe we could ride down there, get distracted some."

"Maybe," Mat said, grinning at the blush flooding his brother's face.

But it wasn't to be. One Eye visited the station again the next day, sending his warriors dashing and darting across the river in hopes of drawing the station crew into a fight in the open. Ben Hunter kept his men under cover, and whenever a Kiowa darted too close, a rifle barked out, stinging the intruder.

Only once did One Eye himself lead the band across the river, and Matt knew this would be a charge pushed to the limit. While the others engaged the youthful warriors, Matt held back. Finally One Eye raced toward the house itself, yelling like a fiend, jumped from his horse, and rushed the door. It flew open, and One Eye himself took a step inside, only to find the path blocked by Matt's big Sharps.

"I'm waitin'," Matt said, gazing deeply into the Kiowa's eyes. "Muerte? Is that what you want, death?"

For the one and only time, Matt read fear in the Indian's eyes. One Eye breathed heavily, then discarded his hatchet. The young warriors withdrew as Matt forced their leader back from the porch.

"Enough!" Matt called, pulling back his rifle. One Eye turned, gazed at his enemy with a mixture of hatred and relief, then raced for his horse and was gone.

"What in heaven's name?" Hunter cried. "You had him cold, Matt! Half the state's been after that man!"

"What's it mean to kill another Indian?" Matt asked. "Plenty have fallen already. They find new leaders. There are many eager to die. This one, One Eye, doesn't waste his men. He respects strength. He won't be back."

"I wouldn't count too much on that," Hunter warned.

But Matt believed it totally. And that, indeed, proved to be the case. Trinity Crossing was troubled no more by One Eye's Kiowas. The warriors continued to burn and raid all along the frontier, but they avoided the dark gaze and long rifle of the devil they knew as Muerte.

As life returned to normal, Matt and his companions finally found time to ride out in search of mustangs. With One Eye loose, the plain north and west of the Trinity stayed free of settlers. It thus provided a refuge for hundreds of range ponies, together with stock run off from ranches farther south. Eli had little trouble locating the band he'd spied in late summer, and in no time Matt's outfit had trapped twenty-five fine animals in a box canyon.

It was a greater challenge driving the horses back to Trinity Crossing. Matt watched the bulk of the herd while Luke, Eli, and Gil ran six at a time back to the corral. It required three journeys over two exhausting days, meaning Matt spent one night alone amid the windswept plain.

Matt slept lightly at first. Then, toward dawn, something woke him. He knew somehow from the veil that draped the moon that he faced grave danger. He made no overt move toward his rifle.

Instead, he drew out a Colt from beside his leg, cocked the hammer, and rose slowly. There before him, glaring down, was the nightmare of the frontier, the scarfaced Kiowa, One Eye.

"Muerte," the Indian spoke bitterly, jabbing Matt's bare legs with the blunt end of a lance.

Matt held his pistol close to his side and waited for the Indian to strike. One Eye made no move. Instead, the surrounding canyon echoed with the whelps of his warriors.

One Eye finally turned the lance and touched it to Matt's chest, letting the point press just enough to draw a spot of blood. Then, screaming wildly, he tossed the lance aside and swung a rifle toward Matt's chin.

"We-ah meeeet a-gain," the Kiowa said, grinning crazily. He then raised the rifle and fired it harmlessly in the air.

"Yes, we're even now, you devil," Matt growled. "Next time somebody'll be dyin', won't they?"

"Muerte," One Eye said, bending down so Matt could see the terrible gash that had blinded one eye. "Muerte."

"Yes, death," Matt mumbled. "It'd almost be welcome, wouldn't it?"

Matt didn't figure the Indian understood, but One Eye turned and Matt thought he detected a grim nod. Then the Kiowas rode off, leaving Matt to await the return of his companions.

# CHAPTER
## ★ 17 ★

From that moment on, Matt never quite had One Eye's Kiowas out of his mind. Ben Hunter insisted a guard be posted at night, and the mere snapping of a twig stirred the entire station to life. The westbound stagecoach carried news that two freighters had been attacked just six miles north of Jacksboro itself.

If further proof of the Indian peril was needed, Matt had only to gaze into the fearful eyes of little Jimmy Peterson. The boy had begun hobbling around on a pair of crutches Matt had cut from willow branches, but his mother feared resuming the journey eastward would cause a resumption of the bleeding. Flora agreed there was no need of hurrying the journey, and Matt in any case was glad the Petersons had stayed. Little Emily had become a fixture of sorts, sitting on the corral rail while the station hands worked the wildness out of their captive ponies and decorating the table with sprigs of purple thistle at dinnertime.

Days passed, and the leaves on the oaks and willows began to put on their autumn cloaks. The midday heat relented, and blankets were needed at night. Matt continued to gaze northward, expecting trouble, but as it happened, One Eye found other game.

Eli was the first to spot the soldiers. Except for their standard-issue Springfields, there was little military about them. Matt responded to Eli's alarm and met the first of the weary, half-naked cavalrymen at the river. In all, twenty-five finally stumbled in, their exhausted leader none other than the celebrated "Colonel" George Washburn.

Little Emily took note of the situation straight away.

"Look, Ma, those men lost their trousers!" she shouted.

"They're near naked," Jimmy added, laughing as he crutched his way to the porch.

Mrs. Peterson promptly ordered her children inside, and they reluctantly complied.

Matt, meanwhile, located a grumbling Ray Calvin at the end of the column, urging the last two stragglers toward the station-house.

"Come on, mules," the sergeant said, prodding the stumbling soldiers with a stick. "You call yourselves members of the Sixth? Poor excuses for crowbait more likely."

Only after the last of the soldiers was escorted to the station-house, and Washburn had taken to the privy, did Calvin explain what had happened.

"Ambushed, pure and simple," the sergeant declared. "We were escortin' supply wagons, four of 'em, when those red devils rode out, wavin' rifles and shoutin' at us. 'Fore I could get to the head o' the column, Colonel Washburn had the lieutenant and half the men chasin' after 'em. Pure fool, that one. Indians ran the men down a ravine, then left 'em to their friends. Ten men gone in the wink of an eye. The rest of us tried to form, but that one-eyed fellow was on us like a blanket, cuttin' up the column, drivin' off the horses, settin' the wagons afire. Lucky anybody got away."

"That wasn't the end of it, though, was it?" Matt asked, staring at the milling survivors. Their bright blue uniforms were notably missing.

"We made camp on a hill, and I set off with young French to find us some help," the sergeant told Matt. "We got maybe a mile when we heard some scattered shots and a considerable amount of wailin'. Well, we hurried back and found the command scattered to high heaven, half o' the boys shiverin' in their union suits, and the camp turned upside down. Got to say one thing for that One Eye. He does a fair job o' things. They stole our blankets, some rifles, mess tins, even most o' the boys' uniforms. Got the colonel's fine coat with the eagles on the shoulders. Only lost two men, but I think that's mostly on account the Indians wanted loot more'n scalps."

Matt gazed at the dismayed company and shook his head sadly. It was an old story, some fool of an officer getting his command shot to pieces. Half Matt's regiment had fallen trying to charge a Yankee battery at Corinth that couldn't be taken. The hardest part, of course, was watching Washburn step out of the privy, minus his coat but otherwise looking ready to greet the President's lady.

"You," the officer muttered when he noticed Matt. "Where's Mr. Hunter?"

"I'm here," Hunter announced, stepping out of the station-house. "What can I do for you?"

"Colonel Washburn, Sixth Cavalry," Washburn said, saluting smartly. "My men are nigh frozen, Mr. Hunter. We need food, clothing, and horses."

"I never in my life sent a man away hungry," Hunter replied. "I suppose we've got some clothes somewhere we can spare. I'll have a look through the boxes of unclaimed freight."

"And the horses?" Washburn asked.

"Well, I don't have any riding horses myself," Hunter explained. "Those in the corral belong to the crew. You'll have to dicker with Matt there."

"Ramsey!" Washburn shouted, glancing around for Matt. The colonel's arrogant eyes settled on Matt, and it was clearly expected the horse trader would respond as a loyal dog and race to the colonel's side. Matt sat beside Ray Calvin and gazed at the river.

"Ramsey!" Washburn shouted again.

"Shoot, colonel, he's the one right over there with Sergeant Calvin," one of the men pointed out. "I expect he can hear you."

Washburn's face reddened as he realized Matt had no intention of responding. Muttering a choice curse, the colonel stomped over and confronted Matt Ramsey face-to-face.

"I need horses," the officer announced.

"I got some," Matt answered with a grin. "Guess just now you don't mind quite so much who you deal with, eh?"

"I need horses," Washburn repeated.

"I've got six saddle-broke," Matt said. "Best thing'd be for you to send word to the fort for some wagons. Some o' those fellows look to be about done in."

"Leave me to worry about my command."

"You done a fine job with it so far."

Washburn stormed away, then reluctantly returned.

"I'll take the horses," he declared. "We'll sign a voucher."

"My brother back home's got a wall plastered with commissary vouchers," Matt responded. "You don't take vouchers when tax collectin' time rolls 'round. Price is thirty dollars a head, cash money."

"Fine gratitude!" the officer raged. "We risk our lives to guard the frontier, and they hold us up like bandits!"

"You don't guard anythin'," Matt argued. "You can't even guard your own pants, it 'pears. This place's been hit hard three times since I been here, and I never saw any bluecoat help tendin' the wounded, buryin' the dead, or chasin' those that did it. You care to buy horses, I'll sell 'em to you. Elsewise, walk back to your fort. It's nigh but twenty miles or so. For all I care, walk to blazes and back!"

It was Matt's turn to stomp off this time. The colonel stood frozen in his tracks.

A few minutes later, Ray Calvin located Matt on the far side of the barn.

"I got boys worn down to the bone back there," the sergeant told Matt. "Ain't their doin' they got a jackass leadin' their company. I'd ask you man-to-man for a horse, but I know that'd leave you holdin' the short end o' the stick. The colonel come up with a hundred dollars, and I figure that ought to buy three horses and hire the others for the day. I'll bring the three we don't keep back to you myself when I bring the wagons."

"Providin' One Eye doesn't get 'em first," Matt grumbled.

"Trust me to know my business, Matt."

Matt was surprised to hear the sergeant address him by his first name. There'd been a grudging respect between the two of them, as often rests between old enemies, but that moment it seemed to have grown into something new—comradeship shared by victims of an equally unjust fate.

"Take 'em, and you're welcome," Matt said, leading the way to the corral. As Eli and Gil brought out the saddle-broken horses, Calvin passed the greenbacks into Matt's hand.

"No saddles?" Washburn called as he stared at the bare-backed horses.

"I can loan you some saddle blankets," Hunter offered.

"You got saddles," Washburn said, turning toward Matt.

"Out here a man's saddle is personal," Sergeant Calvin said, stepping between Matt and the colonel. "I wouldn't loan mine out, colonel, especially if I was apt to need it anytime soon."

Washburn turned to Matt and glared.

"I'll be a while remembering you, Ramsey!" the officer promised.

While Ray Calvin, Washburn, and four of the abler-looking soldiers got atop the horses, Flora Hunter and Mrs. Peterson made their way among the soldiers, offering soup and biscuits, steaming coffee or assorted clothing. The soldiers began to regain bits of their stolen self-respect, and in time they built up a fire and sang old camp songs to fend off a growing chill.

"Fine bunch they are," Luke muttered when Matt slid between the rails of the corral and set out to pick out a new horse to work. "To think they're supposed to protect us!"

"If all the Yankees'd been like that Washburn fellow, we'd have supped in Washington town the first winter o' the war," Eli added.

"They weren't," Matt told them.

Ben Hunter heard the conversation and paid a rare visit to the corral.

"Such talk's no good," the stationmaster declared. "They're on our side now, boys."

"Not mine," Matt argued. "Bunch o' high-nosed Yankees! I got more regard for the dung left by One Eye's ponies than for the whole regiment o' those bluejackets!"

"Well and good, Matt, but it isn't their fault they were born north of the Ohio River. I've got a brother in Iowa served with the Union. Doesn't make him less of a man."

"I got no quarrel with Union men," Matt explained. "These fellows, though, they're the leavin's mostly. Some only signed on 'cause it got 'em out o' jail. Most drink themselves half blind come payday. Look at 'em, Ben. What d'you see?"

"I see a bunch of tired men, some of them wounded, who

have done their best to hold themselves together and do their duty. I saw others of the like in the war, only what was left of their coats was gray. One of them might even have been named Matt Ramsey.''

"Sure," Matt said, tossing a bridle over a speckled gray mustang.

"War's over, Matt," Hunter declared. "It's time you quit fighting everybody and everything."

*If only it was that easy,* Matt thought as he gripped the pony's mane and climbed on its back. *Never is, though.*

# CHAPTER

## ★ 18 ★

As promised, Ray Calvin returned the three hired horses the following day. Wagons arrived as well to carry the soldiers back to the fort. Few words were spoken, and no gratitude expressed to the Hunters for their care and hospitality. It angered Matt, but then he was in a foul mood from his encounter with George Washburn, and greetings from the President of the United States would unlikely have brightened his humor.

"Ought to take this money and ride to Sudsville," Luke said when Matt divided the earnings among the four of them.

"We've got horses to work, and a station to run," Matt reminded his brother. He didn't add what was most on his mind. One Eye remained on the loose, and the notion of leaving the Hunters, Mrs. Peterson, and the children unattended was unthinkable.

And so instead Matt busied himself with the mustangs, and the station continued to host stagecoaches headed east and west. No Kiowas appeared to disturb the routine, and gradually a sense of well-being settled over Trinity Crossing.

Young Jimmy Peterson mended speedily, as was the habit of the young, and together with Emily, the little ones soon got into

anything and everything. Their mother scolded such antics, but
Matt found the guilty smiles and mischievous eyes of the children a salve for his troubled heart.

The Fitzpatricks rode out with Cully Herrick to take delivery
of five horses, and besides providing some welcome cash, the
visit boosted Matt's spirits even more.

A less welcome visitor arrived the initial week of November.
George Washburn and two commissary corporals appeared with
a letter from the post commander at Ft. Richardson.

"You know what it says?" Matt asked as he scanned the lines.

The colonel nodded. Matt beckoned his companions over and
took a deep breath.

"It appears the colonel here's done us a real service," Matt
said, grinning at the irony of it. "Seems his boss was pleased
with our horses, so much so that he's sent these fellows out to
contract another ten."

"Ten?" Luke asked, shaking his head in wonder.

"Well, that's fine news!" Gil exclaimed.

Eli said nothing, just tossed his hat in the air and howled like
a fool.

"I'm authorized . . . ordered to make the arrangements,"
Washburn reluctantly spoke. "Your price?"

"Thirty dollars apiece," Matt said, motioning toward the
horses.

"Seems high," Washburn grumbled.

"I've got a few you could have for less, but I wouldn't put a
soldier on their backs," Matt explained. "You could be in for
some hard compaignin', and for that you need an animal that
can outlast old One Eye himself. Mustang're suited to that sort
o' labor. These ponies'll graze on dry buffalo grass if there's no
oats, and they'll not break down on you when the trail's full o'
rocks and ravines."

"I'm authorized to pay twenty," Washburn replied.

"I get twenty-five from the liveryman in Jacksboro," Matt
countered. "An' he's close to family. I mostly sell him the
smaller mares and geldin's, too. You need animals to carry a
man, his weapons, and a field pack. Thirty's my price. Your
buyers know they'd spend more'n that for broken-down nags
over in Millstown."

"Your horses aren't shod," Washburn pointed out. "That will
require some effort on our part."

"I had a smith with me before," Matt said, gazing icily into Washburn's eyes. "You remember him. He was a bit bigger than me and considerably darker about the face."

"Heard he got himself shot," Washburn said, smiling as he watched the words cut into Matt's heart.

"Lots o' good men been shot lately," Matt replied. "Some made the mistake o' followin' fools."

Washburn turned abruptly as if to leave, but one of the corporals cut off his retreat.

"Colonel, the letter," the soldier said.

Matt waved the paper in the air, and Washburn's face glowed fiery red.

"We'll meet your price," Washburn mumbled. "Get the animals ready."

"You got three hundred dollars?" Matt asked.

"You'll get your money, Ramsey!" the colonel shouted.

"When you get your horses," Matt promised. "Meanwhile, it's best we make out a contract o' sorts."

"You have my word on it," Washburn said, extending his hand toward Matt.

"Rather have it in writin'," Matt told the corporals.

"My hand's better than any contract ever drawn," Washburn said.

"We'll see," Matt said warily.

"You've got Colonel Stanton's letter," one of the corporals pointed out. "I assure you it's a serious offer. When can you make delivery?"

"Horses're here," Matt said, pointing to the crowded corral. "You bring out the money, they're yours."

"I'll tell Colonel Stanton," the corporal promised.

Washburn then turned his horse and led the way toward the river without speaking another word. Once the soldiers had splashed across to the southern bank, Matt tossed his own hat into the air. His companions shouted their good fortune, and soon the whole station was alive with laughter and celebration.

That night, seated around the dinner table, the mustangers discussed what use three hundred dollars could be put to.

"It's enough to buy a place of our own," Luke said, closing his eyes a moment and grinning wildly as he imagined it. "Maybe out on the Brazos, where there's still good open range. Longhorns roam free over half the Llano, and it wouldn't be so hard for the four of us to put together a decent herd, drive 'em to Kansas next summer, and get rich.''

"We could build us a house," Eli suggested. "Paint the walls yellow like my place back home."

"We'd have feather beds, too," Gil added.

"It'd be a big place," Luke said, smiling dreamily. "With plenty o' room for family."

The others orally constructed the ranch. Matt listened and tried to recall doing the same. He'd charted the future but once, with Kate, but they'd never envisioned anything half so grand.

Flora Hunter surprised them with an apple pie that had emptied the sugar tin as well as the apple barrel.

"We get few chances to celebrate," she announced. "Seems fitting. You boys have sold your horses, Jimmy's discarded his crutches, and we've had no more trouble from the Indians. It seems the proper time to slice some pie and shout a little."

"Amen," Ben agreed. "Now, can anybody around here dance? I've got the urge to lead my darling in an old-fashioned reel or two, but we need some company."

"Miz Peterson?" Gil said, offering his hand.

Emily skipped over and tugged on Matt's sleeve, and the fourth pair was the least likely of all, Luke and Eli. Until, that is, they could persuade Gil to surrender the hand of Mary Peterson. Ben Hunter called the beat, and the lot of them pranced around the floor, whooping and bowing and stepping as lively as any New Orleans dandy.

Matt thought the only thing missing was a fiddle, and he regretted old Stump Riley wasn't along. He hadn't thought of Stump in quite a while, and he mused sadly that the dead ought to stay buried in memory as well as in the earth.

"Come on, Matt," Emily complained as he slowed his step a bit. "Do it like Luke!"

Matt laughed and tried to cast old Stump's grizzled features off into memory. But the more they danced, the more he recalled the cantankerous old cuss.

It was well past dusk when they finally grew weary of the dancing and collapsed into chairs or on the floor. Matt huffed for breath and fought back an overwhelming fatigue. Emily brought over a glass of lemonade, and he gulped it like a man left months on the desert.

"I'll be dancin' soon, too," Jimmy declared as he sat on his mother's lap. "My leg's gettin' well, Miz Flora says."

"She'd know," Matt declared.

"Got a dandy of a scar," Jimmy claimed.

"Imagine so," Matt said, remembering the bloody mess that had been the youngster's leg.

"It won't be the only scar if you don't hurry along to bed now," Mrs. Peterson said, lifting Jimmy high onto her shoulder and beckoning Emily along. The girl nodded obediently, paused only to give Matt a quick kiss on the cheek, then trotted off to bed.

Ben Hunter made his way to the cupboard and fetched a bottle of peach brandy kept for special occasions. He poured out six glasses, and Flora passed them to the four exhausted station-hands.

"To health and prosperity," Hunter called, raising his glass.

"Yours and ours," Matt agreed, touching the rim of his glass to Luke's. The others did the same, and the room filled with the pinging of glass on glass until each cup had touched its five fellows. They then sipped slowly, letting the brandy spread a rare warmth through chests too long frozen with pain and gloom.

"You won't leave before spring, of course," Hunter said, re-filling the glasses.

"Winter's a fearful time on the plains," Matt answered. "And we wouldn't leave till you had a crew hired on anyhow."

"To friends," Hunter called, and again the room filled with the ping of glass on glass.

"To the mustang, wildest cuss alive," Luke proposed when a fresh bottle refilled the glasses.

"To the longhorn, even meaner," Eli called out, teetering when the glasses were raised a fourth time.

"To Cap'n Washburn," Matt said when the last of the brandy was dribbled in his own glass and that of Ben Hunter, the others by now peacefully dozing as they lay. "Fool and jackass, but reluctant founder of our good fortune."

Hunter barely managed to sip his brandy, for the toast elicited a great roaring laughter.

"Hope One Eye doesn't pay us a visit tonight," the station-master said, sinking dizzily to the floor. "An old squaw could scalp the lot of us."

"And most'd never feel it," Matt added, likewise collapsing.

The candles illuminated the room until they exhausted themselves, leaving a half-dozen lumps to snore away the night. They awoke to find daylight streaming in through open windows, the Peterson children peering at bloodshot eyes, and the sound of bacon frying in a nearby skillet threatening to explode their eardrums.

"Had ourselves a regular full-blown whing-ding of a time last night," Luke said, covering his ears as if that would halt the ringing in his head.

"Good thing we don't celebrate too often," Matt added. "Likely kill the lot of us."

Gil and Eli nodded their agreement while Flora helped her husband into a chair. Mrs. Peterson brought welcome cups of coffee.

With clanging head and rumbling stomach, Matt began to pay the price of merrymaking. Still, he couldn't recall when he'd danced and sung and drunk with equal abandon.

*Thank the Lord I won't do it again anytime soon,* he thought.

# CHAPTER

## ★ 19 ★

It proved too early to celebrate. The same morning Ben Hunter put the Petersons on the eastbound stage, Max Clancy rode in with a dozen Bar C cowboys.

"Heard you were out here, Ramsey," Clancy said, gazing with seasoned hatred at Matt. "Also heard you planned to sell horses to the army. Well, that'd be a big mistake."

"Oh?" Matt asked, tapping his fingers on the wooden grips of the Colt that seemed permanently affixed to his hip since departing Fitz's livery.

"I'm th'only one hereabouts does business with the soldiers," Clancy boasted. "Am I right, boys?"

"Right as rain, boss," the cowboys shouted.

"Now, the deal I'll make you is this. I hear from town you plan to get thirty dollars a head for your animals. Well, I'll split it with you, give you your half now, and do the deliverin' myself. How's that for fair?"

The cowboys laughed. Matt muttered, "Stinks close to as bad as you, Clancy," and pulled the rancher from his horse. In seconds Matt had an arm clamped around Clancy's throat.

"Best let go o' him," a tall, shaggy-haired cowboy urged as

he nudged his horse toward his struggling employer. "I got a fair eye with a gun."

"So do I," Ben Hunter declared, appearing in the station-house doorway with a rifle.

Gil, Luke, and Eli scrambled over from the corral, and before anyone quite knew what had transpired, the Bar C hands dismounted and dove into the midst of the mustangs.

Matt first attended to Max Clancy. The rancher had years and close to a forty-pound advantage over Matt, but easy living had softened muscle, and blows that once would have sent Matt reeling on his heels were now deflected with ease. Matt, in turn, landed two quick rights and then added a well-directed toe that connected with the falling Max Clancy's forehead.

What followed was an old-fashioned free-for-all in which young mustangers and dusty cowboys exchanged insults and slammed fists against jaws. Teeth were dislodged, and flesh was bruised and gashed. At first, cowboy and mustanger squared off in pairs. Men wrestled each other to the ground, flailing away wildly. Then, as the tide turned against the cowboys, their shaggy-haired leader ordered those not directly engaged to lend a hand to those in trouble. Numbers began to show, and Matt angrily faced a trio of young hands who, except for their allegiance, might have been Luke's twins.

*Well, so much for fair fighting,* Matt thought as he dipped his shoulder, grabbed a handful of sand, and hurled it at the three encircling wranglers. Then, snatching a length of oak from a nearby woodpile, Matt clubbed the confused cowboys to the ground and set out after fresh targets.

"Good Lord, look at Matt!" Luke gasped as he grappled with a two-hundred-pound hulk of a ranchhand. Matt's log quieted the cowboy rather easily, though. Soon those Bar C hands still able slunk off toward their waiting horses and tried to sort out the cobwebs occupying their craniums.

Matt thought to throw a rope around the lot and drag them through a considerable length of the Trinity, but an ear-splitting cry drew his attention to the south bank of the river.

"Indians!" Alder Thomas, the eastbound's driver, screamed, and Matt kicked loose from the grasp of a cowboy and hurried toward the stationhouse. Flora tossed him the Sharps, and Matt raced wild-eyed toward the river as the coach thundered in, its side peppered with arrows and torn by bullets.

"Look, Max!" one of the cowboys cried as One Eye formed a band of a dozen or so Kiowas on the bluff opposite the station. The stage roared on into the shallows, completed its crossing, and rolled through the open doors of the barn.

Matt's arrival, big-bore rifle in hand, seemed to deter immediate pursuit. The Hunters ushered a shaken Mary Peterson and her fearful youngsters inside. Luke led a second woman and two boys in their early teens along to the house while Gil and Eli offered rifles to a pair of gentlemen passengers.

"Well, this is rare convenient," Max Clancy declared, motioning his battered crew toward him. "Got plenty o' amusement today, it seems."

"We could use your help," Hunter said, pointing to the Indians.

"Well, it'd suit me just fine to let 'em chew on you a time," Clancy said, "but it so happens this particular batch has given me a bad time of it. Come on, boys. Let's shoot us some Indians!"

The cowboys mounted their horses and headed north, away from the gathering Kiowas. Matt stared bitterly as One Eye raised his hand and waved his companions toward the station. There was nothing for Matt to do but race back to the house and join the defense.

"Curse that Clancy," Matt muttered as he raised the Sharps and fired. The lead rider crashed into the river. His death seemed to stir the others to life, and amid bloodcurdling screams, the Kiowas charged.

From house and barn, a terrible fire greeted the Indians. Yellow flame erupted from rifle barrels, and pistols blasted projectiles so that the air seemed to buzz with the whine of lead. Three horses fell, and two Kiowas howled in pain. The rest jumped from their mounts and raced toward the house or sought shelter in rocks or behind troughs or woodpiles.

Matt expected a desperate fight, but it didn't happen. Clancy had merely been biding his time. He now made his own charge, catching One Eye's band in the rear and flank. Cowboys unloaded pistols into the backs of their trapped quarry. A few Kiowas managed to break away and make a wild rush for the Trinity. Most returned fire as best they could, singing their death chants as the tide of violence overwhelmed them.

Matt felt his legs tremble as he looked on the scene of utter slaughter. A pair of boys no older than his brother Bucky rose from their hiding places and stood, bare-chested and calm, as onrushing riders laid them low. One Eye also looked upon the scene with a dying heart. The scarred face lost its color, and his arms waved frantically in an effort to extricate his band from the trap, but he was powerless to fend off enclosing death.

Matt was strangely drawn to the Kiowa. There was something oddly familiar in the hollow gaze of that single eye. Here was a man who had also lived with death and defeat, a man refusing to yield to inevitable destruction.

"You can't fight fate," Matt whispered as he crept from porch to water trough, past fallen Kiowa youngsters as he continued into the trees. There he came upon the old warrior, shielding two wounded youngsters from Clancy's attentions.

Matt had the urge to continue, to give the old foe death from a respected source. But the shaggy-haired cowboy got there first. One Eye leaped to one side and plunged a lance through the surprised cowboy's chest. Max Clancy then raised a rifle, took aim, and sent three bullets from a Henry rifle exploding through One Eye's back.

The Kiowa didn't drop immediately. Instead, he leaned on his bloody lance, mumbled a chant, and gazed in death toward Matt Ramsey. A hundred yards away, Matt thought he heard the dying lips mutter, "Muerte." Then the lips formed what might have been described as a smile when the solitary eye glazed over. One Eye fell to the ground and was quickly overrun by Bar C hands.

The two wounded Kiowas made an effort to protect the stricken body of their leader, but rifles soon closed those eyes. Matt was too far away to hold back the knife Max Clancy drew from a boot scabbard.

"Look here, Ramsey!" Clancy called, bending over and applying the knife eagerly. "This is what I do to those who get in my path!"

Matt felt his knees weaken as Clancy held up a handful of raven-colored hair. The rancher then bent over One Eye again.

Matt turned away and stumbled to the river. The moans and cries of the wounded haunted the air. It was a scene from hell, a vision of madness. He wished at that moment to be anywhere other than where he was.

Luke found Matt kneeling beside the river, washing his hands over and over again.

"Matt?" his brother called.

"I got to get the blood off," Matt said, plunging his wrists into the mud and thrashing them about in the water.

"Matt, there's nothin' there," Luke said, grabbing Matt's shoulders and pulling him away from the river.

Matt stared in surprise. Couldn't Luke see the blood? It stained his fingers, clung stubbornly to his arms. Matt would never cleanse those hands!

"It's all over," Luke whispered, leading Matt toward a fallen tree. They sat there together for a time while Luke explained the Bar C company had moved on, leaving four of their number behind.

"Eli? Gil? Ben?" Matt cried.

"Not a scratch among 'em," Luke said, sliding a comforting arm around Matt's shoulder as Matt himself had done the day their father died. "Matt, folks're worried. Little Emily's howlin' for fear you've come to harm."

*I have,* Matt thought, blinking away a tear.

"We can't stay out here forever," Luke said. "There's work waitin'. The coach wants a fresh team, and the front o' the house is shot up fair."

Matt nodded. "Yes, work's waitin'," he whispered.

Luke helped him rise, and Matt slowly, somberly made his way toward the house. It wasn't patching pine or hitching horses that drew Matt, though. No, he set about a grimmer task.

It seemed eerily prophetic that a spade should be resting beside the front door of the stationhouse. As Emily Peterson hugged Matt's leg, and Eli offered a comforting nod, Matt took the spade and turned toward the clump of rocks that concealed One Eye, or what remained of him.

"Matt, I'll tend to that," Ben Hunter said, reading the mixture of grief and rage blended in Matt's blazing eyes.

"Got to," Matt explained, unable to elaborate. How would Ben understand, for instance, that only labor could fend off the encroaching fingers of madness? They couldn't see the red stains, couldn't hear the echoing cries of the fallen that had haunted Matt before—after Shiloh and Corinth, in the cold, gray nights trudging homeward from Vicksburg. No, they didn't know, couldn't imagine, the terror that could visit a man.

Matt began at the river. The fallen cowboys lay there, elbow to elbow. Matt gazed sadly at the holes in their stockings, at the trouser pockets turned inside out, at the shaggy-haired fellow's bare lower half. Their comrades, too hurried to dig a hole or share a moment of prayer, had taken the time to remove boots and valuables, even trousers.

"Rough company you kept, boys," Matt spoke to the younger of the slain, youngsters too bright-eyed and fuzz-cheeked to have been fit company for the likes of Max Clancy. There'd be no names to etch on picket crosses.

"Well, at least your trial's over," Matt said as he scooped dirt with the spade. It was right somehow that they would share a markerless resting place, those four nameless cowboys. To Max Clancy, they were something you bought and used like new boots or cartridges. Feelings and honor brought no profit!

Matt dug and dug. He carved from the earth a deep trench, a slit a good four feet deep. The hard rock below prevented a deeper grave, but even so, it was a far more elaborate burial than any of those cowboys would have expected.

Luke and Eli helped lower the bodies. Burying even the likes of that shaggy-haired devil half bare seemed wrong, and Luke wrapped a worn saddle blanket about the cowboy's bare middle.

When the last of the slain were placed in the trench, side by side so none would lay atop another, Matt filled in the hole. Eli stomped down the turned earth, and Luke rolled boulders over to prevent wolves from getting at the corpses.

"This was the easy part," Eli said as Matt turned toward the rocky clump. "Matt, maybe we can take a turn."

"I got to," Matt said, shaking loose of Eli's grasp.

Matt chose a slope overlooking the river and shaded by a pair of tall oaks for One Eye's Kiowas. The ground there was hard, unyielding. It seemed even more appropriate, for so was the man who would rest there. The spade rang eerily as it struck rock, but the grave widened and deepened and took shape.

Matt had no notion of the killing done that day, though. His completed trench had no hope of offering the Kiowas such respectful treatment as was extended their slayers. As Luke, Gil, and Eli brought the bloody corpses to the grave, Matt shrank back in horror. There weren't four or five as he'd supposed, but a full dozen. The ones killed near the stationhouse seemed froen in timeless sleep. Except for holes in chests or bellies or foreheads, the Kiowas seemed little different dead than alive.

The others had suffered at the hands of Max Clancy. Every scrap of clothing had been torn off as souvenirs, and two of the older men had fingers cut from hands.

"Rings," Eli muttered. "Saw 'em do it."

One boy who could have been no older than ten had hair, ears, and toes cut away. Two had been mutilated more horribly. Matt nodded approvingly as his young companions lowered the bodies into the grave, taking care that stiffening arms were placed respectfully across chests. One Eye was the last.

"It wasn't necessary," Matt said as he stared at the jagged slices torn from the Kiowa's body. From the chest down the proud warrior was barely recognizable.

"Hope they're proud," Eli mumbled bitterly.

"Were braggin' about it," Luke noted. "Well, fate settles such scores, I figure."

"Yes," Matt agreed, gazing at the haunting, hairless head of the man who had so often spread terror across the frontier. Matt then bent over and closed the single eyelid.

"Wish I knew somethin' to say," Eli remarked. "Don't know any Kiowa words."

"Matt?" Luke asked.

"A sad day, old friend," Matt whispered as he shoveled earth over the silent figures. He considered the others likely thought the words directed at them and not the man who would soon be swallowed by earth and darkness. *You're at peace now,* Matt added silently.

Rocks were again rolled atop the grave, but Eli had the notion to arrange them in the shape of an arrowhead.

"A remembrance of sorts," the young man declared.

Matt thought it appropriate. The buffalo left their hides behind. Except for those bits of flesh carried away by Clancy, the earth would soon digest all of One Eye. And if, in later years, the shape of the rocks changed, as often happened, Matt thought it only appropriate. No monument outlasted the memories of its constructors, after all.

# CHAPTER
## ★ 20 ★

The last of One Eye's Kiowas were brought past Trinity Crossing three days later. Three boys, none of them much over five feet tall, had been rounded up by the Sixth Cavalry. They rode thin ponies flanked by soldiers. A wagon carried the bodies of others who had chosen to make a fight of it.

Colonel George Washburn, leading the column, paused long enough to boast of his victory.

*Some triumph*, Matt thought. *Must be proud o' fightin' little kids.*

With the colonel was Max Clancy.

"Of course," Washburn said, "you well know Mr. Clancy here played a role in quelling these raids, too."

"Put an end to most o' them Kiowas my own self," Clancy claimed. "I got ole One Eye's scalp danglin' from my bedpost, not to mention a few other momentos here and there."

Matt turned away, disgusted. Clancy wasn't finished, though.

"Heard about your contracts yet, Ramsey?" the rancher called.

"What about 'em?" Matt asked, stopping at the corral.

"Tell him, George," Clancy said, grinning at the cavalryman beside him.

"Seemed there was a mistake made by the commissary clerks," Washburn explained. "Reports weren't filed correctly. Colonel Stanton was sorely put out, said he needed mounts now! Well, my friend Max here stepped in and took over the contract straight away."

"I don't understand," Matt said, knowing enough to realize the cackling colonel and devious rancher were enjoying themselves at his expense.

"I warned you," Clancy said. "Your contract, if you ever had one, has been cancelled."

"That right?" Matt asked Washburn.

"I told you before," Clancy barked. "You got stock to sell to the army, you deal with me!"

Washburn nodded, and Matt scowled.

"I guess that says somethin' 'bout the value o' your handshake, Washburn. And your word. As for you, Clancy," Matt added, gazing icily at his old enemy, "I'd sooner sell my horses to the devil than deal with you."

"Oh, you'll come around, all right," Clancy said with confidence. "I can be patient. You can't."

"I've got more time than you do," Matt argued. "And I've got a letter from Colonel Stanton. Man sounds like he might care to know how his orders have been sidetracked. Might be worth a ride into town to see the fellow."

"Might be the last ride you ever took," Clancy threatened.

"I've known trouble before," Matt reminded both men. "Clancy, you've twice put me at odds with you. First time it cost you a brother. Last time, as I recall, you didn't fare a lot better. You remember the feel o' my arm tightenin' on that sour throat o' yours?"

"I remember everything!" Clancy growled. "You remember somethin', too. That darky friend o' yours got his reward, and you should've got yours. You stay at cross purposes with me, and I'll have your scalp opposite that Kiowa's. Hear?"

"What I hear's somethin' makin' wind," Matt answered. "Now get clear o' here before I take it in mind to give you the drubbin' you deserve."

"He's under my protection," Washburn insisted.

"I figure your Colonel Stanton'll settle accounts with you,

Washburn,'' Matt declared. ''Why don't you hurry those prisoners into town 'fore they break loose and steal your trousers? Ever get that coat back, colonel?''

Washburn's face reddened, and he set his jaw hard. A brusque wave of his hand had the column in motion.

Matt didn't bother watching them leave. Instead he hurried to the corral and began saddling the big black for the ride into Jacksboro.

''Stage comin','' Eli called, and Matt abandoned his plan. The westbound splashed past the departing soldiers and pulled up to the station.

''You and me, Gil?'' Matt said, pointing toward the barn.

Gil nodded, and the two of them set off to bring a fresh team of horses for the coach.

If Matt had ridden directly into town, it's possible the trouble that followed might have been avoided—at least for a time. As it was, seven riders led by a steel-eyed dwarf of a cowboy arrived only half an hour after the westbound pulled out again.

''Afternoon,'' the frail-looking cowboy called. ''I'm Ned Brewster. I come to talk with Ramsey.''

''Which one?'' Luke called.

''Didn't know there was but one,'' Brewster answered, ''but you don't appear to be him, sonny. I'm lookin' for an older fellow with dark hair.''

''That'd be me, maybe,'' Matt said, stepping out of the barn.

''It's him, all right,'' one of the cowboys declared. ''Tell him, Ned.''

''Mr. Clancy sent me with a greetin','' Brewster explained. ''Said to tell you to turn over them ten horses the soldiers want. I'm to pay you a hundred and a half for 'em. Now.''

''I don't take orders from Clancy,'' Matt replied.

''You'll take your orders from me!'' Brewster shouted. ''Less you care to find an early grave. Hear me?''

''I told Clancy when he was here I'd sooner deal with the devil,'' Matt said. ''I haven't changed my mind.''

''Don't need to,'' Brewster said, grinning broadly. ''The devil, you say? Well, mister, meet him in person.''

Brewster gazed down with eyes as cold and heartless as a coiled rattlesnake. His thin lips tightened as his mouth formed a kind of snarl, and the fingers of his right hand fondled a pistol.

''Devil, huh?'' Matt asked, stepping closer. His eyes narrowed, and he concentrated on Brewster's hands. "I got a name, too. Kiowas give it to me. Muerte. Know it?"

"I look Kiowa?"

"It's Spanish," Matt explained, coming closer. "Means death. I deal it out like cards at a poker table. Ask Bob Clancy."

"So, you're that one," Brewster said, nodding with a begrudging kind of respect. "Well, I give you credit for gumption. It'll get you killed, though. Likely you don't know o' me, but I figure somebody'll fill you in. I got a name folks remember."

"Oh?" Matt asked.

"Ask around some. I'll give you some time to think things over."

"Why bother?" Matt asked.

"Call it a courtesy," Brewster explained. "Just know that when I come back in the mornin', I'll expect those ponies waitin' and ready to go. Understand?"

"I'll do no such thing."

"You don't know a way to make a thing easy, do you? Well, let me spell it out simple. Max ain't got ten horses to deliver just now, and if he did, those commissary fellows'd know straight off they weren't the same ones they looked at here. Max figures to pay you fifteen dollars for 'em, you know."

"And collect thirty?" Luke asked. "He's crazy!"

"Oh, he's got more sense'n you'd think, sonny," Brewster assured them. "Fact is, he'll have 'em one way or another. I could take 'em right now and save the hundred and a half. Folks'd get killed, though, and Max don't really take to inconvenience. Might be some questions asked. So you have 'em ready for me tomorrow, understand?"

"You're not goin' to do it, are you, Matt?" Eli asked.

"Man can't just ride here and take our property," Luke added. "We fought 'em before."

"Oh, that was just a sort o' gettin' acquainted talk," Brewster explained. "This is serious business. I'll have those horses."

"Only one way to get 'em!" Eli shouted. "Through me!"

"That'd slow us down what, a minute or two, boys?"

Brewster gazed at his companions, and the seven of them laughed chillingly.

"You've had your answer," Matt declared. "Now leave!"

"Till tomorrow," Brewster said, turning his horse and leading the way to the crossing. "Enjoyed meetin' you, friend."

"You come back tomorrow, you'll enjoy it a good deal less!" Matt vowed.

Once the riders were gone, Matt's companions gathered around to voice their outrage. Eli and Luke were vocal. Gil remained quiet, though.

"Gil, you look worried," Matt observed. "Somethin' wrong?"

"Plenty," Gil confessed. "I seen that fellow before, Matt, only I can't figure out where."

"Could be anywhere," Ben Hunter said as he joined the group. "Wichita, Kansas. Red River camps. Ft. Worth and Dallas. Was in Jacksboro when I saw him at work."

"At work?" Luke asked.

"Shot three men in two days," Hunter explained. "He's quick as lightning, Matt, and he's got all the nerve of an alley cat. The army ran him out of Sudsville 'cause he shot a corporal. Judge Waxman vowed to see him hung if he came back."

"He's a killer," Eli said, frowning.

"I've seen him do it," Hunter went on. "He'll square off with you, Matt, kill you dead."

"And if I don't take the challenge?" Matt asked.

"You will," Gil muttered. "I remember it now. He did away with a fellow up in Cooper, Kansas. We were through there this summer, remember, Luke? Eli? Some fellow wanted to buy out the mercantile, and the owner, well, he didn't want to sell."

"Yeah, I remember," Luke said grimly. "One night we heard shots. Shopkeeper had a little girl. Well, he didn't have her after that night. She took a bullet in the head, fired through her own window. Was sleepin', Matt. Nobody saw, but everybody knew."

"Mercantile changed hands the next afternoon," Gil grumbled. "Shopkeeper had three girls, you see."

"I don't," Matt declared.

"You got a brother," Eli said, gazing nervously at Luke.

"And friends," Hunter added. "Is it such a loss to take, a hundred fifty dollars?"

"Isn't the money," Matt said, glumly gripping his pistol. "Once you start backin' down, there's no end to it. I don't know I could stomach belongin' to Max Clancy, and that's just what it'd be. You know that, Ben."

"Then it's face Brewster," Luke said, picking up a rock and

tossing it against the wall of the barn. "No, Matt. Better to take the horses and head west right now."

"You can't run from trouble," Matt argued. "I know that much. It catches up with you in time. Thing to do is plan for it, get your thinkin' straight. We'll settle it tomorrow, all right, but it'll be on our terms."

"How so?" Eli asked.

"To begin with, we set 'em at ease. . . ."

Matt began by sketching a map of the station in the sandy ground, then explained what was to be done. The others listened attentively. But in the end, Ben Hunter asked the one hard question.

"What about Ned Brewster? He's the kind to take us all on and wind up with the winning hand!"

"Only fightin' his way," Matt argued. "A fast hand, hard eyes, they're fine when you go after a man. Even better if he comes to you. But they won't be much help in this kind o' fight. It's cold-hearted nerves and a good eye with a rifle that'll carry the day, and we've got plenty o' both."

"He'll have help," Gil reminded Matt.

"Sure, boys mostly who know how to move a cow 'round a pasture, but who've never pressed home much of a fight. They got little to gain. Clancy won't be payin' them bonuses to get killed, will he? Some'll recall the boys killed at the river, too, how they got themselves picked over like a stray calf circled by buzzards."

"I don't know that I like it much," Hunter grumbled. "The eastbound's due around ten, and . . ."

"Don't like the notion much myself," Matt admitted. "But as for the stage, take my word for it, they'll know the schedule. Last thing Ned Brewster wants is extra eyes around. He'll come early so he can catch the sun at his back. And we'll be ready an' waitin'."

# CHAPTER

# ★ 21 ★

Matt rose before dawn. As he dressed, he stared eastward toward the beginnings of that new and fateful day. Brewster would soon arrive, and there were preparations to complete.

He didn't disturb the others. Better they should sleep a bit more. Rest steadied the nerves, improved the aim. As for Matt himself, well, he was on familiar ground, wasn't he? Less understood was Max Clancy.

"Why?" Matt whispered as the sun cracked the far horizon. It wasn't personal. Some men might have set after their brother's killer with impassioned vows, but Clancy was a cold type, and every move was calculated with the precision of a Swiss timepiece. Oh, the money he'd make from selling horses was a part of it, no doubt, but there was more. Max Clancy had a hunger for feeling powerful.

*Yes,* Matt thought as he remembered the rancher's grinning face when holding One Eye's hair toward the sky, *Clancy was the kind who liked to stand atop a hill and revel in his conquests.* And that, Matt knew, was why Ned Brewster would have company that morning.

As daylight streaked over Trinity Crossing, the others began rolling out of their blankets. A chill November bite was in the air, and they shivered and hurried into their clothes. Matt felt another cold, too—the icy touch of impending death.

He said nothing as Gil and Eli hurried to feed and water the horses. Luke slipped out the door and hurried toward the hog pen. By now Flora had bacon crackling on the stove, and Ben stepped out onto the porch with a grave frown. Matt met the stationmaster at the corral.

"Maybe they'll think it over a bit," Hunter suggested. "Let us stew awhile."

"Soldiers won't wait forever for their horses," Matt grumbled. "And anyhow, I don't figure Clancy for a patient sort. He'll be along."

"Brewster will, you mean," Hunter muttered.

"Oh, Clancy, too. Fellow likes to see what his money's bought him."

"You've done all this before, haven't you?" the older man asked, shaking his head. "Don't see how you hold onto your nerve. I hardly slept last night, thinking of Ned Brewster starting after Flora. How do you think it will go?"

"A long time ago, I stopped tryin' to figure things," Matt replied. "They'll come. We'll do our best to stop 'em. It's a throw o' the dice, Ben."

"I don't see how you stay so calm about it."

"Frettin' doesn't much help," Matt said, gazing over at Luke, who was busy filling the hogs' slop trench. "Don't know if I've said it, Ben, but I'm obliged for you takin' us on. More'n that, for standin' by us this mornin'. Some might've shown us the road."

"I guess I know where debts are owed," Hunter answered. "I still recall you and Eli riding through those Kiowas when I thought we'd all be dead before sundown. Don't get me wrong, Matt. I'm not a brave man. My knees are shaking, and I fear I'd lose any food I put in my stomach."

"Yeah?" Matt asked, managing half a smile. "I hadn't noticed."

He stepped inside the stationhouse then, accepted a cup of steaming coffee from Flora, and collected the guns and began breaking them down. An oily rag and ramrod cleared away accumulated powder, grit, and sand. Matt twirled cylinders until they whirred silently. He assured himself the firing pins were sound. Finally, he began loading fresh cartridges in each chamber, placing caps on the pistols, and lining up shells for the newer Springfields.

When all was in readiness, Matt strapped on his pistol belt, stuffed the extra revolver in back, then cradled the Sharps, and set off to visit the others. Like Matt, they'd hardly touched their food. Unlike him, their foreheads wrinkled with worry. And whether tapping fingers on corral rails or kicking rocks about the sandy road that separated stationhouse from barn, they responded to anxiety with action.

Matt recalled how the colonel had walked the line at Vicksburg, had steadied the younger men with a hand on trembling shoulders and shared a tale with the grim-faced old-timers. Matt now did the same.

"High sky this mornin'," he told Eli.

"Be glad when the sun chases off this chill," the young man replied.

*Sun's got nothin' to do with that kind o' cold,* Matt thought.

"That little mare's comin' along just fine," he told Gil at the corral.

'Yeah, she'll prove a dandy," Gil agreed. "Thought we might hold onto her, let her breed us some good colts when we get down to the Brazos." They shared a far-off smile that was all too fleeting.

Matt greeted his brother last of all.

"I never quite been in a scrape like this," Luke confessed. "Could be we'll get ourselves killed this time."

"Bucky'd be mighty disappointed," Matt observed. "Sure as sunrise, he'll expect to winter with us. That house gets mighty full with those yappin' youngsters o' Amos's."

"Yeah," Luke said, grinning. "I can just see him settin' fire to the cat's tail again."

"What?"

"That cat little Pauline sets such store by. Fool critter likes to find a man's drawers and scratch 'em to slivers. Buck spread a little coal oil on the fool thing's tail while it was sleepin', then set it afire. Never did see anythin' howl like that cat!"

"I never held much with torturin' animals," Matt said, shaking his head in disapproval.

"You never had your personals torn up by that cat," Luke replied. "Didn't do much other than singe the tail a bit anyway. Afterward, that cat sure did give us a wide berth, though."

Matt couldn't help laughing as he envisioned his younger brother pranking the cat. Then he turned away to complete his preparations. Water buckets were set out along the walls of house and barn to combat flame, and a shallow trench was dug beyond the corral as a last line of defense. Matt knew it would serve about as much use as the rocks where One Eye sought refuge. Out in the open, numbers would tell, and that was one ace Max Clancy held. The other was Ned Brewster.

The Bar C riders appeared at the river a bit short of nine o'clock. The mist that usually clung to the bank had cleared, erasing any chance of an ambush at the crossing itself. Brewster led the way, followed by eight cowboys, each in varying states of nervousness. Max Clancy brought up the rear.

Matt motioned his companions to their posts. Luke and Eli took the front window of the stationhouse. Ben Hunter guarded the door. Gil climbed to the barn loft. Matt stood beside the half-open swinging doors below, Sharps in hand.

"I come to get the horses," Brewster called.

For a second Matt thought of the his jittery companions, of Ben Hunter's admitted fears. Were the horses so important that men should die over them? Was anything?

"I'll just be gettin' 'em now," Brewster said, laughing as he waved a pair of young cowboys toward the corral.

"No, we'll be holdin' onto 'em awhile," Matt finally answered, swinging the Sharps over so as to discourage the cowboys. Both immediately retreated to their comrades, leaving Brewster alone to face Matt.

"Fool's move," Brewster observed. "Get you killed like as not."

"Nobody lives forever," Matt answered.

"Well, I admit I was gettin' awful bored, Ramsey. Man needs a good fight to sharpen his teeth."

"You'll get one," Matt promised.

Brewster paused a moment, gazed back at Clancy, then turned and retreated.

*Keep ridin'*, Matt prayed. *Lord, let him keep on goin'.*

But it wasn't in Brewster's character to step away, and Matt watched as Max Clancy stared at the barn, forming a wicked smile with his crooked teeth.

"Ready, Gil?" Matt called to the loft.

"No, but I figure I won't be this time tomorrow, either."

*I'll settle for you bein' alive tomorrow,* Matt thought as he steadied his aim. He concentrated on Brewster, but the killer was too sly to lead the way. The cowboys left their horses, then fanned out in an enveloping circle. Only when each had reached cover a hundred yards from the station buildings did Brewster wave them to advance.

The Bar C hands showed no great eagerness to close with riflemen, and Matt hoped the Sharps would add to their reluctance. The big-bore rifle was best at dropping buffalo, and its first shot shattered its target's hip and sent the man to the ground, wailing in pain.

"They got Rod!" another cowboy cried.

Instead of unsettling the line, though, the shot sent the surviving wranglers rushing forward. The Springfields barked, and another man went down. Gil dropped a third from his perch in the loft. Now, though, Brewster knew where to strike. He raced toward the woodpile while Matt feverishly reloaded. Then, jumping to his feet, he opened up with a pair of pistols on the stationhouse.

Splinters flew from the shutters and door. Someone cried out in pain, and Matt detected a shrill whine from Flora Hunter. Brewster waved two companions toward the house, but when they kicked the door open, a shotgun blast threw them back onto the porch, their chests opened by buckshot.

"Max, bring up the rest!" Brewster urged.

*The rest?* Matt thought. He spotted one cowering behind an oak. The other two made their way to Brewster's side. Clancy himself had seemingly vanished.

"Climb on down, Gil," Matt shouted.

Gil made his way down the ladder from the loft, and Matt left the young man to guard the barn. There was but the one way into the place, and Gil had proven a steady enough man.

Matt rested the Sharps beside the door, then slipped outside. He raced along the barn, then crawled across the open ground toward the corral. The house remained frozen in deadly silence, and as he fingered his twin pistols, he envisioned Luke and Eli bleeding out their lives on the hard floor beside the window, saw Ben Hunter staring lifelessly at his beloved wife.

An urgency powered Matt's legs, and he sprang forward, raced past the startled mustangs, and slammed hard against the side of the house. His charge had surprised Brewster, who fired without taking aim and thus missed.

"Hello, the house," Matt called.

"There's a welcome sound," Hunter answered, coughing. "We got 'em on the run, Matt."

"Luke?"

"He's shot up some," a sputtering Eli Lyttel explained. "Matt, there's three of 'em back o' the woodpile, and two more in the trees."

"I'll tend to 'em," Matt promised. He slipped back around the rear of the house, anxiously searching out his enemies. A nervous cowhand, no doubt sent on the same flanking mission by Brewster, suddenly appeared.

Had the youngster not hesitated, he might have lived. Matt never flinched as he unloaded on the wrangler. Two shots slammed into his chest from ten yards away, and the cowboy simply collapsed in a ball of agony and expired.

"Marty?" Brewster called. The silent answer told all.

"Ned?" Max Clancy then shouted from the distant trees. "What's happened, Ned?"

"It's gone sour!" Brewster cried, the first trace of panic entering his voice. "That's what's happened. Get up here and lend a hand."

Matt continued his approach to the woodpile. At last he could see the remaining antagonists. Clancy and a slightly built cowboy stood twenty yards distant on either side of an oak. Brewster and another man remained at the woodpile.

*If only I had the Sharps,* Matt lamented. The long rifle would have put a neat hole in Max Clancy's forehead and ended the duel. As it was, the Colts would have to do the trick.

"You spot him, Max?" Brewster cried.

"Back o' the house, I think," Clancy said. "Can't say for sure. He's a snake, that one."

"Those boys you sent to the livery should've done the job right first time out!" Brewster complained. "Be a close thing now!"

Matt thought so as well. He edged his way closer, thought to rush the rear of the woodpile and open up, but that would suit Ned Brewster fine. And if Brewster did fall, Clancy would have a fine shot at Matt's back.

"He's good at aimin' in that direction, too," Matt muttered

as he mused about the Jarvis brothers. So Clancy hadn't forgotten his brother as supposed!

There was but one window on the back of the stationhouse, and it was shielded from the inside by a massive oak shutter. As Matt considered a different approach, the shutter slid upward, and Flora Hunter greeted him.

"Figure you can get through here?" she asked.

Matt gazed cautiously behind him, holstered his guns, and climbed inside the house. The shutter slammed down with a bang, and Flora ushered Matt toward the front room.

The stationhouse was a shambles. Bullets had showered the room with splinters, shattered dinnerware, smashed bottles on the counter. Eli stood at the window, his left arm bound in a bandage torn from the back of his shirt. Luke rested against the wall a foot away, moaning as pain worked its way through him. A bunched cotton apron soaked up blood from his bleeding shoulder, and a tighter binding covered a second wound on Luke's left thigh.

"How are you holdin' out?" Matt called.

"Dandy," Ben answered. The side of his face was splashed with glass fragments, and one arm hung useless at his side. A shotgun rested in the other.

"Glad you're here," Eli said, mustering a smile. "They're still at the woodpile, Matt."

Luke didn't speak, but his eyes gazed grimly at his brother. Matt felt a rage well up inside him. He reloaded the empty chambers of his pistol, then turned to Flora.

"Any way onto the roof?" he called.

"Figured you'd come around to that," she said, grinning. "Trap door just at the head of the stairs. Pops right into the attic, and there's a door of sorts cut into the eaves."

"No way onto the roof proper?"

"You won't need it," Flora said grimly. "That door's right over the woodpile. You can't miss."

"I'd have gone myself," Ben claimed, "only, well, Flora did a fair job with this scattergun before, but . . ."

"If you missed, Ned Brewster'd be out there," Matt finished the thought. "He won't be for long."

Matt climbed the narrow stairs leading to the half-storey second floor. It was there the Hunters made their quarters. Ben had an office of sorts up there, too. It was intended to house guests, but the low ceiling offered little comfort. Matt had to hunch over until he popped the trap door open. Then he climbed into the musty attic. The door, held shut by a double latch, was straight ahead.

Matt took a deep breath and drew both pistols. He would finish Ned Brewster then and there if he had to pounce on the killer. There was another one, too, Matt reminded himself. Then, with fingers that steadied with firming resolution, Matt opened the twin latches and kicked open the door.

The sound startled Brewster, but he responded quickly, raising a pistol and peppering the swinging door. Matt ducked back inside as splinters cascaded through the attic. Brewster's companion stepped back to get a clean shot at the would-be bushwhacker. Then the Sharps barked.

Gil hadn't been idle. He'd seen everything, and one shot was enough to rid the countryside of another Bar C hand. Brewster rushed to the cover of the woodpile, and Matt sprang at him.

It was over ten feet to the ground, but Matt never hesitated. The woodpile was there to break the fall, as was Ned Brewster. The killer jumped clear, though, as Matt landed in the midst of the stacked oaks, collapsing the pile. Even before landing, though, Matt had fired his pistols.

It had been impossible to aim while flying through the air, but at three feet, it was hard to miss. One bullet shattered Brewster's kneecap, and a second pierced his side and cut its way through one lung. The killer rolled free of the falling logs and raised his own gun as Matt fired a third and final shot into the small man's forehead. For a second Ned Brewster's face froze in a gaze of surprise. Then both eyes rolled back, and the killer died.

"Ned?" Clancy shouted as he scraped away soil in hopes of digging a trench beneath the oak.

"Keep diggin', Clancy!" Matt yelled. "Dig your grave!"

The words struck the rancher like well-aimed darts. More to the point, they sent the remaining cowboy racing for his horse. The slight-shouldered wrangler leaped atop the nearest animal and galloped toward the river, howling as if a devil were in close pursuit.

He was. But not after that cowboy.

Perhaps it was the fiery look in Matt's eyes, or maybe it was the ghostlike sound of his voice. Something sent Max Clancy retreating. And Matt, recovered from his collision with the woodpile, followed.

Some strange sort of irony led Clancy toward the river, to a strangely formed pile of boulders that seemed to offer a final refuge. Fingers fumbling with a revolver, Max Clancy called for help from cowboys who were no longer among the living.

"Bob?" he shouted. "Where are you?"

"Waitin'!" Matt screamed as he wove his way through trees and rocks fifty, then forty feet away.

Some sort of madness took possession of the rancher then. He saw the prowling horses, five, six of them stomping nervously, each back carrying an empty saddle that offered salvation.

"Here, boys!" Clancy pleaded. "Here!"

Whatever caused Max Clancy to fire his pistol, it was not the thing to do. The horses were upset to begin with. Years of weaving between the nasty horns of longhorn cattle had taught them to be wary, and the gun duel had sent half their number fleeing into the river. Those remaining reacted at once to the gunshot, turned, and raced away. Their escape was blocked by a stand of willows, though, and they turned, swept back by the invisible hand of fate. Or perhaps justice.

Clancy welcomed them.

"Here, boys!" he cried as the horses thundered closer. His eyes lit with hope as he discarded his gun and raced toward the nearest animal. Then, hope fading to be replaced by cold fear, Max Clancy turned from the raging hooves of the stampeding beasts.

Matt watched with no satisfaction as a billowing dust storm rushed at the rancher, then swallowed him whole. Matt listened as horseflesh collided with humanity, as heavy hooves crashed down, shattering bone and crushing vitals. And when the horses completed their wild charge and the dust settled, only a muddle of crushed bone and distorted flesh remained of Max Clancy.

Matt didn't bother to stand triumphantly over the corpse, and he took no souvenirs. He rubbed the bruised side of his ribcage and hurried toward the house. The door swung open, and Eli fell against Matt's chest.

"Luke?" Matt called as he squeezed Eli's good arm.

"Is it over?" Luke asked, his weary eyes fighting back pain.

"Yes, little brother," Matt answered. "All over."

# CHAPTER

# ★ 22 ★

t wasn't really over, of course. There were bullets to extract
rst. Then the grim task of burying the dead awaited.

Matt tended Eli first. Of late the young man had seemed so
much older than the trembling fourteen-year-old who had clung
o Matt's side the eve of the dreadful hanging. Now, as he cut
ad from Eli's arm, Matt saw only another boy hurried into
manhood, his heart pounding beneath a hairless chest.

"We should have put another dram of whiskey into him,"
Flora grumbled as Eli's face twisted in pain. He whimpered,
nd Flora ran a motherly hand across his young brow.

"He's known pain before," Matt said as he drew out the
humbful of lead and placed the sizzling brand against Eli's arm.
he young man cried through gnashing teeth as flesh blackened
nd blood vessels closed. Flora then bound the wound while
Matt turned to his brother.

"My turn?" Luke whispered.

Matt nodded, then helped his brother rise. Flora and Ben eased
Eli onto a waiting mattress, then washed the table down.

*Strange*, Matt thought as he lifted Luke. *He's not heavy at all.*

After all, how long had it been since Matt carried the boy aroun
on his shoulders down at the creek? Or was that Bucky?

Flora provided a stiff cup of rarely-touched Irish whiskey, an
Luke sipped it slowly. The spirits soon overpowered him, fair
as he was from loss of blood, and Matt set to work.

The shoulder came first. There was scarcely any flesh there t
speak of, and the bullet was easily located. Matt removed it a
well as a splinter of bone. Again the brand cauterized the wound
and Matt examined the thigh.

Matt's fingers touched the discolored flesh, felt the warm rus
of his brother's blood. Tears Matt thought would never agai
form blurred his vision.

"Steady, son," Ben advised, dabbing Matt's face with a cloth
"It needs doing."

Matt nodded and probed the wound. The bullet proved eva
sive, had lodged beside the bone, and Matt had a time removin
it. Flora applied the brand, and Matt huddled beside his trem
bling brother, silently praying that time would mend flesh an
erase recollection.

With the bleeding halted, Flora bandaged Luke's thigh, an
Matt carried his brother to a second mattress. Luke and Eli la
in blissful ignorance the remainder of that troubled day whil
Matt set out to dig another grave.

Not all the Bar C villains required a resting place. Gil ha
escorted three of the more fortunate into Jacksboro where a
eager Judge Waxman ordered them jailed.

"That judge says he's holdin' three hundred dollars for you i
town as well," Gil explained upon his return. "Our frien
Brewster was wanted up in Kansas, it seems, and there's a fa
reward."

Matt frowned. It seemed a sad commentary that equal valu
should be placed on the death of a scoundrel and the autum
labor of four men.

"I'll give you a hand with the hole," Gil offered, strippin
away his shirt and taking the spade from Matt's blistered hands
"How're Luke and Eli?"

"Restin'," Matt explained. "Eli's apt to be up yappin' 'for
supper."

"And Luke?"

"Be a time gettin' back his strength, but Ramseys come o
good stock. He'll mend."

"Sure he will," Gil declared. "We all will."

Matt wasn't so sure. When he resumed digging a quarter-hour later, he felt a dark shadow hovering close by. Haunting voices seemed to call, "Muerte. Muerte." Matt again sensed a kind of choking madness. It was not held off by the sight of the four empty-eyed cowhands stretched out at the edge of the grave. What remained of Clancy lay as before, the rock arrowhead pointing accusingly at its mangled face. Gil had wrapped Brewster in a saddle blanket, the judge insisting proof of the killer's demise would have to be provided to the authorities.

Matt would have thrown Brewster in with the others and hang the reward, but Gil, practical about such matters as always, insisted the money would provide the fine acreage they'd so recently dreamed of.

"That's deep enough, don't you figure?" Gil called when the trench cut three and a half feet into the earth. "They'll get along to hell on their own without you helpin' 'em there."

Matt nodded, tossed the too-often-employed spade aside, and climbed from the grave. The two of them then laid the bodies of the slain cowboys side by side. Finally, with a rush of uneasiness, Matt grabbed the stiffening hands of Max Clancy and dragged him to the edge of the crater. Gil nudged the rancher's corpse over the edge, leaving it oddly facing down into the earth while his companions gazed upward.

"Maybe we should turn him over," Gil suggested.

"No, he's headed in the right direction," Matt mumbled bitterly. "Cover him up."

Gil filled in the grave while Matt dragged himself to the river. He shed his clothes and bathed the dust and sweat and dirt and blood from his weary body. It didn't erase the bitterness or the pain death's shadow had brought, though, and when he emerged from the water, even the fresh clothes Gil brought failed to revive in Matt a sense of restored humanity.

Early the next morning, Matt rose sleepily to discover Sergeant Ray Calvin and a squad of soldiers waiting beside the corral. Judge Waxman and a deputy sheriff were along as well.

"Colonel Stanton wants to know if he can have his horses," the sergeant explained when Matt appeared at his side. "Seems somebody told him a tale or two about you sellin' 'em elsewhere. I got a bank draft coverin' the contract right here."

Matt took the paper, stuffed it in his pocket, and gazed at the horses eagerly stirring in the corral. Gil appeared, and together with a pair of soldiers, they picked out the promised ponies and turned them over to the army.

"I'll have a like amount for you as well," Waxman said when he examined the stiff form of Ned Brewster. "Was a little fellow, wasn't he?"

"Big enough, I expect," Matt muttered.

"Well, we'll have to have some photographs taken. Care to pose with him?"

Matt's blazing eyes answered for him, and Waxman nervously motioned for the deputy to tie the corpse onto the back of one of the mustangs.

"Plan to stay in these parts?" the judge asked.

"No," Matt replied. "We'll see Ben through the winter, I'd guess, then head out."

"Prudent of you," Waxman observed as he mounted his horse. "Never pays to acquire a reputation, you know. And killing can get to be a habit."

Matt frowned and nodded.

"Glad you came through your trials," Sergeant Calvin said, extending Matt the courtesy of a sharp salute and a friendlier grin. "I imagine we'll have more business for you."

"Mustangs, he means," Gil added as Matt stared darkly toward the graves.

"Sure," Matt said, returning the salute in his casual, Southern style. "You watch yourself, sergeant."

"Always do," the cavalryman explained as he led his men and their newly acquired horses along. "I'd take that draft to a bank soon, if I was you. We ain't been paid lately."

Matt couldn't help brightening as the soldiers struck up a bawdy tune. They rode to the river, splashed across, and vanished on the far bank, taking Waxman, the deputy, and their grim bundle with them.

Matt drew the bank draft from his pocket and showed it to Gil.

"Looks like we've turned a profit, Mr. Ramsey."

The title hung awkwardly on Matt, and he shook it off with a motion of his head as he walked to the stationhouse and made his way to Luke's side.

"Thought maybe you'd gone off and left me, like when you

and Kyle joined the army," Luke whispered as Matt squeezed his brother's hand.

"You know I'd never leave you to enjoy all this rest and sympathy on your own."

"You won't write Ma and Pa about it, will you?"

Matt frowned. The fever had likely clouded Luke's thinking.

"They've gone away, remember?" Matt whispered.

"They're dead," Luke muttered as a wave of recollection swept over him. "Flora says I'm doin' just fine, you know. Plans to knit me a sweater, she says, and Eli one, too."

"Maybe I should've let 'em shoot me some, too," Matt suggested.

"Nobody 'round to cut out the bullet," Luke said, forcing a grin onto his face. "Can't worry about things, Matt."

"What things?" Matt asked as Luke released his grip and rested the fingers of his good hand instead on Matt's shoulder.

"The killin'," Luke whispered. "You only did what you had to do. Wasn't any other path to take."

"Wasn't there?"

"You know there wasn't."

"That doesn't make it any easier, Luke."

"Maybe not, but I guess sometimes you just don't have a lot o' choices. Like ole One Eye. Nothin' to do but stand your ground."

"And die?" Matt asked.

"And live," Luke argued. "I been doin' a lot o' thinkin' about our ranch. After a time, I figured to find myself a little yellow-haired gal, one who can cook and sew and tend things. Like Flora over there."

"She fires a shotgun fair, too," Matt pointed out.

"Likely I'd need someone to bring me to my senses now and then. Later on, we'd have a dozen youngsters to chase through a creek and teach to hunt and swim."

"I had that sort o' dream once myself," Matt said, sighing. "Dreams're for younger men, though."

"Not always," Luke objected. "That ranch would be a fine place for all of us. Maybe you could even . . ."

"What?"

"Forget. Start over. Find whatever it was you lost when you went off to war."

"It's too late," Matt grumbled.

"You figure Kate'd want you moanin' in your sleep, talkin' to dead Indians and mopin' around? Not a chance, Matt. She'd take a broom to your hide and straighten you out."

"It's not just Kate," Matt explained. "There's Ma and Pa, Anna Louise."

"So what'll you do for them, roll over and die? Matt, Ma'd want grandkids and a house full o' prankin' and prayin' and singin'. You know that. You remember all those old yarns Pa used to spin. One thing I know from 'em. Ramseys never quit on anything, especially themselves. Shoot, I know I'm just a kid really, and a shot-up one at that, but I know you can't go on cryin' over somebody forever. I hurt, too, but first chance I get, I'm ridin' to Sudsville. Comin'?"

There was something terribly inviting about the glow in Luke's eyes. It was contagious. Matt blinked, and the shadows passed away as if the noon sky had erased them from the landscape.

"Got to ride to town in a few days anyhow," Matt said. "Need to cash this draft at the bank while it's still good."

"Might wire Bucky, too; tell him we got room for him this winter."

Matt smiled. It would be good to have the prankster around, as good as it would be to have Luke back on his feet. Wounds would, after all, heal. And perhaps hearts also, if given the chance.

*It'll never be like before,* Matt knew. Kate, Ma, Pa, they were gone. But maybe there was something waiting out there, perhaps down south on the Brazos. He hoped so.